MW01059585

live
for
me
Blurred Lines #2

live for me

Blurred Lines #2

ERIN
New York Times Bestselling Author
MCCARTHY

Copyright © 2014 by Erin McCarthy

All rights reserved. No part of this publication may be reproduced, stored in or introduced into a retrieval system, or transmitted, in any form or by any means (electronic, mechanical, photocopying, recording or otherwise) without the prior written permission of the copyright owner and the publisher of this book, excepting brief quotations used in reviews. Purchase only authorized editions.

This is a work of fiction. Names, characters, places, brands, media and incidents are either the product of the author's imagination or are used fictitiously. Any resemblance to actual events, locales, organizations, businesses or persons, living or dead, is entirely coincidental.

Cover © 2014 by Sarah Hansen, Okay Creations
Interior Designed and Formatted by

E.M.
TIPPETTS
BOOK DESIGNS
emtippettsbookdesigns.com

more books by
ERIN McCARTHY

Blurred Lines Series

You Make Me

Live For Me

Let Me In

Meant for Me

Breathe Me In

The True Believers Series

True

Sweet

Believe

Shatter

For a full list of over sixty books available visit:

www.erinmccarthy.net

www.facebook.com/ErinMcCarthyBooks

prologue

"GET OUT," MY GRANDMOTHER SAID, wheezing as she reached for her glass of water. "I can't stand to look at you. Sometimes I think you were born to punish me."

I didn't respond, even as the pain squeezed my heart, and defiance burned inside me. I could never get used to her hatred, could never understand what I did to deserve it. And part of me would always want the approval she would never give. But I had learned a long time ago that protesting or trying to soothe her only made her angrier, even when I wanted to tell her precisely what I thought of her treatment of me.

So I started towards the kitchen to be out of her line of vision.

"No. I don't mean get out of the room. I mean get out of my house. For good."

I paused, my back to her. Interesting. She couldn't mean that.

Yet if I knew one thing, it was that she never made a threat she wasn't prepared to keep. I waited, on high alert. I spent most of my time with Gram in a half-present fog. I could care for her, clean the house, cook, all with my mind far away. Her slurs, her taunts, her demands were white noise, an emotional ceiling fan I could tune out as it whirred around and around me.

"Pack your stuff. *Now*."

The fan had shut off suddenly.

Those words snapped me out of my usual state of determined ignorance, complacency. I turned slowly, studying her, gauging her seriousness. Her face was red and she looked furious. I wasn't sure what had sent her over the edge, but she was definitely not hurling the words just to hurt me. She meant it.

"Is that what you want?" I asked. "If I'm not here, no one is going to take care of you." It wasn't a taunt. It was the truth.

"I should have left you at the orphanage. I swear, it's your fault I'm sick. You're probably poisoning me, for all I know."

That was enough of a poke to have me speaking before I could stop myself. "If I wanted to poison you, you'd be dead already," I told her simply. Hell, I could have killed her six times over since I was in charge of both feeding and medicating her.

Sometimes, despite what was smartest for survival, I just couldn't keep my mouth shut.

In pure rage, she threw her plastic tumbler at me, but she was weak from her emphysema and it fell short of its mark, water splashing up over both of us. "There's always been evil in your heart, Tiffany. It's because your mother opened her legs for that low-class man from down there."

Down there meant anywhere south of us in Maine. My father

2

had been from New York City. Not that I'd ever met him. But I'd heard nothing but slurs, both racial and otherwise, against him. How my mother's life was wrecked by him and their mutual drug use, and consequently my grandmother's as well. Because I was born. Ironic, considering neither woman had retained full custody of me for very long.

I'd lived in thirteen houses in eighteen years, including a brief stint with my mother as a baby and twice with my grandmother for a few years after my mother died. This last time had been mostly as her makeshift nurse. Now when she struggled to stand in her anger, her bulky weight preventing her from getting any lift off the sagging couch, I automatically reached out to help her.

She slapped at me. "Don't touch me. You have thirty minutes to get out of here or I'm calling the cops."

Drawing my hand back, I admit I felt a strange sense of relief. It sucked to know that your own family didn't give a damn about you, but it was nothing new. And in getting tossed out I could finally be free. Free of her. Free of hope that she'd ever care, but free nonetheless.

Being alone would be worth the ability to walk and talk without fear of criticism.

To live an actual life, not just one in my head.

And this time, I wasn't coming back.

It only took fifteen minutes to pack my life in a duffel bag and a backpack, and then I pulled on a coat and hat, her cursing me the whole time from her floral sofa throne. She had ruled over me from that sofa for four years, with a meaty fist and a sadistic need to punish me for my mother's mistakes.

"God hates selfish sluts."

live for *me*

I stared at her, unblinking, wondering why she didn't see the ridiculousness of what she was saying. I had never been a slut, and I'd had no opportunity to be particularly selfish either. I never left the house. "Does He?" I questioned, in an act of defiance that I couldn't resist. "How does God feel about hypocrites, I wonder?"

She gasped, her mouth falling open to hurl a scathing comeback at me.

I didn't wait to hear it.

Since my dignity was all I truly owned, I held my head high and left.

The screen door slammed shut with a bang behind me and I turned, looking back at the house that had never been a home. It was run-down, Grammy's finances having seen better days. Winter was early to the party as usual, and it was windy, cold outside. Damp. The paint was peeling on the clapboard and the house seemed to hang on like Gram did, defiant, sagging, stuck on this island off the coast just to be obstinate.

I wanted to cry, but my eyes were dry. I'd had too many exits to feel much of anything. It wasn't the first time I didn't know where I was going next, but it was the only time I actually controlled that future.

Part of me wanted Gram to come to the window, to watch me leave.

She didn't.

I walked away, down the drive.

chapter
one

"SO THIS IS YOUR ROOM," Hattie said, turning the knob and pushing open a door.

I peered around the older woman, curious, palms sweating, heart beating unnaturally fast. When I saw a bright cheerful room with a sunny yellow bedspread, I was speechless. For the first time since my grandmother had tossed me out on my ass two weeks earlier, I actually felt my throat close, had my vision blur as I struggled for composure.

"It's really nice," I whispered finally when the smile started to slip on her kind face in alarm as she watched me. "Too nice."

Too nice for me. I'd never had my own room.

She laughed, a kindly, warm laugh. "Nonsense! If you're going to be living in this big old house by yourself when Mr. Gold's not here, you should get a decent room. Not that there are any bad rooms." She led me inside and pulled back the soft white drapes, revealing a set of French doors. "But being on the first floor is nice because you have this private patio."

I actually felt like I was going to be sick, a weird sort of panicked excitement that overwhelmed and nauseated me. This couldn't be real. Or if it was real, it was going to disappear instantly. Fighting the urge to actually pinch myself, I set my duffel bag down on the dark hardwood floors next to the bed and followed her to see the view. It was the ocean. Beyond that shore was the island I'd grown up on, Vinalhaven. The sight stilled my panic. I could still see home.

Yet for the first time in my life I was going to be alone. Completely and utterly alone, in the best way possible.

Based on a recommendation from my high school teacher, I had landed a job as the caretaker for some rich dude who was never there.

Best. Job. Ever.

Once I got used to the silence, I figured it would be like chocolate meets a hot shower meets winning the lottery, with the check handed to you by a super-hot guy.

I was anticipating peace, with no foster siblings messing with me and trying to brush up against me or offer me help getting dressed.

No yelling. No backhanded cracks to my face. No Gram demanding care all day long, some necessary tasks, some simply spiteful.

If this room and this carefully manicured private terrace were any indication, it was going to be paradise. Like a vacation from being me.

"It's beautiful," I murmured, as we stepped out onto the

terrace, and I breathed in the salty, briny air of the ocean. "Are you sure you want to quit this job?"

She laughed again, and it amazed me how easily she laughed, how often she smiled. "Yes. Absolutely. I want to go spend time with my grandkids. Besides, I couldn't stand the quiet being in this big house by myself. I swear, I about jawed the landscapers to death every week all summer." She gave me a look of concern. "Are you sure you want to do this? It's a lonely existence. Mr. Gold is only here once or twice a year, at most."

Perfect. The less he was there the better, in my opinion. Being naturally curious, I had done quick online research on him, and discovered he had paid over two million dollars cash for this property, and that he was a music producer in New York City. The record label had nicknamed him Gold Daddy, because of the volume of hits he had produced. I was picturing an overly tanned guy in his sixties who wore sunglasses inside, even at night. Not who I wanted to hang out with.

Lonely would be a welcome change from continual harassment. "That's fine with me. But why does he have a house he never uses?" I asked, because it seemed crazy to me. As Hattie had led me through the house, the formal living and dining room furniture had been covered with sheets to keep the dust off and the whole house felt very still, empty. Well cared for, but not well loved.

"He doesn't like to come here anymore. Not since..." She shook her head. "Well, never mind that. He's just busy in New York."

So she didn't want to share the boss's secrets. I could understand that, but since she was no longer working for him, I was surprised. It meant Hattie really was as good a person as she seemed. But it did increase my curiosity about Mr. Gold.

"And you're sure you can handle keeping the house clean? It's really just dusting and sweeping and then dealing with the kitchen and your bathroom."

I touched the bush in the pot next to the door, to see if it was real. It was so perfect it looked fake. But it was real.

Like this house. Like this job.

The place was huge, the biggest house I'd ever been in, but I didn't think that it was anything I couldn't handle considering no one was living in it and most of the rooms were shut up. I'd cleaned at Gram's, plus cooked for her and fetched and carried. I'd walked to the grocery store, paid the bills. Taking care of an empty house with zero clutter would be easy, as would the solitude. It was more that I was worried about damaging something. As we had walked through the mansion I had been overwhelmed by its grandeur, and when I bumped an end table in the foyer, I almost had a heart attack. I had eyed the electronics in the grand family room with excitement and horror. I wanted to explore everything, but was afraid to touch.

At least in front of Hattie. Once she was gone, I planned to poke into every dark corner in an effort to feel less intimidated by the quiet, the hulky furniture, the blinking lights on the technology present at every turn.

This terrace, despite its elegant green potted bushes, felt cozy and contained, the view totally amazing. I could see sitting there and feeling comfortable. Not like I belonged to the house, but like I could visit in peace.

"I just can't get over how young you look," Hattie said. "I'm going to fret about you being here by yourself. Thank God for security systems."

It was hard not to be sensitive when people mentioned my looks. I was vertically challenged, to say the least, and I had big brown eyes that were too large for my face. In my opinion, anyway. By sixteen I'd given up thinking that I was going to have some sort of late bloomer growth spurt. I did look young, and I hated it. "I'm eighteen," I said, hearing the defensiveness in my voice.

"To me, eighteen is infancy," she said with a chuckle. "Honey, I have bras that are older than you."

That was a visual I didn't need, giving Hattie's billowy chest. But she was being really kind to me and I felt guilty for sounding a little snotty. She hadn't meant it as an insult. So I gave her a smile. "I'm probably smaller than your bras, too. I kept waiting to shoot up, but it never happened. I'm pocket-sized."

"You have an advantage, you know. Everyone must want to hug you and take care of you."

That almost made me laugh, but she was so sincere I resisted the urge. No one had ever taken care of me, and yet here I was. I had survived, intact. Mostly normal. Suddenly panic was replaced by excitement. I was on my own. I had a future. A real one. With no rent and no interference, I could save my paychecks to go to community college and get a nursing degree like I wanted. The life I had thought was going to drone on endlessly, the same, day after day caring for Gram, was now suddenly all changed, and it sent a wary anticipation through me.

When Hattie reached out and hugged me, I was startled, but I didn't resist. In fact, I sank into the embrace, taking in her floral

9

scent. Despite it being so chilly outside, her touch was warm and comforting.

"If you need anything, you have my cell phone. Plus I'm just down the road for three more weeks before I go to Florida."

"Thank you," I said, closing my eyes briefly, wondering how it was that some people were lucky enough to be born to women like Hattie, and others were not.

Like me.

Somewhere I had a father who might or might not know I even existed, and a mother who had died without seeing me for three years. And Hattie was moving several thousand miles to be near her family.

There was a whole flurry of last minute directions, suggestions, and concerns, and then Hattie left.

I was alone.

In a house the size of my high school.

After unpacking my few clothes into my new room, I wandered the mini-mansion, figuring out how to turn on the touch-sensitive lights, and jumping when I approached the refrigerator for water and it told me the weather in a disembodied voice. Forty-two degrees Fahrenheit, partly cloudy. In the hall bathroom designated for me, I found a shower with six shower heads and a jetted tub. And there was high speed Internet. I could click on my Tumblr account and see everything in less than a second. Glorious. At Gram's I could make a sandwich waiting for pages to load.

By five I was grinning as I flopped on the overstuffed sofa, a soda in one hand, a doughnut in the other. Hattie had told me to eat whatever I wanted. There was a restock list I was to shop from each week with household funds. I might have exaggerated my driving abilities. As in, I had none. No driver's license either, so I wasn't going to be taking the truck that was sitting in Mr. Gold's garage for the caretaker. I would just ride my bike, like I always had, and he would never know.

The house had to be ready at all times for an unexpected appearance from Mr. Gold, and he had a sweet tooth. Chocolate éclairs were to be kept fresh and ready to go in his mouth on a moment's notice.

I liked the rich guy already. His never-used house rocked my socks off and his fridge was nirvana. I wondered what happened when he didn't show up three hundred and sixty days out of the year. Who ate the éclairs, the Canadian geese in the yard? Crazy. Rich people were flat out nuts. But screw the geese, I was eating the doughnuts now. Alone.

Yet as the hours crawled by, it felt more and more alien to be by myself. What had seemed so awesome, the ability to talk really loud just to hear myself, and rolling around on fat plush furniture, and taking random bites of various junk food, gave way to an overwhelming silence and a queasy stomach. I turned the TV up loud because the remarkable quiet was unnerving.

I could feel and hear myself breathing.

I swear I could even hear dust drifting down onto the furniture. By nightfall, I had turned on every light within reach, and flicked on three ceiling fans, despite the cold temperatures outside. The fridge said it was thirty-nine degrees now. Camped out in the family room at the back of the house, I peered through the glass of the windows in the darkness, my reflection and everything around me clearly outlined. There were no blinds, no drapes. I felt totally exposed.

A minnow in a fishbowl.

Even squinting, I couldn't see into the dark beyond the multi-tiered terrace to the lawn, and beyond that the ocean. If there were someone out there, I would never know. Yet they would see me, quite clearly.

When the sun was shining earlier, I had only thought about how amazing it was to slide over the wood floors in my socks, in complete blissful solitude.

Now in the dark of a blustery Maine nightfall, Richfield felt too large, too empty, too exposed. Still.

Yep, the house had a name. Who did that?

Guys whose last name was Gold.

Mr. Gold of Richfield Hall. Was that irony or what?

A man so rich he could own a house he never came to, just because.

Clutching my cell phone, I decided to turn off most of the lights so I wouldn't be so visible from outside. Wearing a tank top that I'd had since I was fourteen and was too small, thus proving that I had in fact grown despite my fears to the contrary, I tugged the bottom of the shirt down for the tenth time in an hour and moved around the family room, flicking off a half dozen of the lamps I had turned on during the high of my newfound independence. No one to holler at me if I wasted electricity. But now all I could think was that Hattie was right- it was a big house.

I had mistaken assumed only old houses made creaking noises. Richfield was only five years old, but the wind hit the windows with an ominous straining sound, and at random intervals the floors seem to pop and groan.

Cat was texting me and I was grateful for the interruption. After Gram had kicked me out, I'd stayed with my one-time foster sister and best friend. Only friend, honestly. Bouncing from foster house to house didn't lend itself to lasting friendships. Cat and her boyfriend Heath took me into their house in Vinalhaven, but I had known I couldn't stay long. I needed to find some way to support myself, and their lovefest didn't need me around. They basically smoldered at each other on a regular basis, and I rolled my eyes so many times I almost knocked myself over backwards. I was happy for them. I just didn't need to see how in love they were repeatedly in the form of their casual groping.

But despite the dumb luck of landing this job, I was glad to know they were both still close by, and happy that Cat was sending me stupid YouTube videos of cats falling down stairs. I smiled as I sat on the couch in the mostly dark room and watched as a cat made the most godawful screeching sound at a dog on my phone screen. The dog barked back.

And kept barking when the video stopped.

I sat up straight, heart thumping. There was a dog barking outside.

Not good. Because who did it belong to? And why was it barking?

I figured I could either sit there and wait for it to stop, or for the intruder the unknown dog was barking at to break into what was supposed to be an empty mansion. Or I could get up and see what the noise was about. Being practical, I shoved my cheap cell phone in my pocket and moved to the hallway, planning to go to the cabinet Hattie had shown me that housed the owner's hunting rifles. They weren't loaded, but I did know how to shoot.

I could at least lift it as a threat if necessary. Debating calling the cops, I stopped in the hall and listened carefully.

Nothing. No barking.

I dismissed the idea of calling the cops. Years in the foster care system had proven to me that while there were great officers, there were also those who were bored and bitter, who didn't give two shits about a teen girl, and would be annoyed that I had interrupted their TV viewing to go out and investigate a whole lot of nothing. I was about to go for the rifle cabinet when the front door swung open without warning and I froze, debating which way to run.

"God, it's bloody cold out there for October," a man said as he entered, presumably to the dog who ran into the house alongside him. In shadow, the man stamped his feet on the doormat, drawing up short when he saw me. "Who the hell are you?"

chapter
two

I FELT TRAPPED UNDER HIS SCRUTINY, nowhere to hide. Nowhere to run. He'd used a key on the front door so this was no burglar. I swallowed hard. "I'm Tiffany." Then because I had a sick conviction this was undoubtedly the owner of Richfield, I added, "Sir." I had no clue how to speak to a rich dude but it seemed like I should be respectful. I wished I hadn't left the box of doughnuts carelessly on the coffee table in a sticky disregard for his expensive property.

"And where do you come from, Tiffany?" He sounded mildly curious, nothing more. He had a low, smooth voice, masculine.

"Vinalhaven." The black dog ran over to me, sniffing at my leg, and I bent over to pet his silky coat, gauging him to be a Lab. "Hey, buddy," I murmured.

"Where is that?" the man asked, divesting himself of his coat and tossing it on the end table.

"It's the island across the way."

"That craggy looking island? Where like twelve people live?"

I nodded, shoving my hands in my pockets self-consciously.

"Ah," he said. "That explains it."

Explained what? But he stepped into the light from the family room then, and I lost the ability to speak. My question shriveled up and died on my lips. If this was Mr. Gold, and I had to assume it was, he was not sixty-five years old, botoxed, or dressed like a pretentious douchebag.

He was more like thirty. Sexy. Wearing what looked like expensive but ordinary jeans, a plaid shirt, a bag in his hand. An overnight bag. He had strong features, an angled jaw, and hair that was carelessly too long, varying in color from dark brown to caramel to sand, though it didn't look done in a salon. Either he had a hell of a hairdresser, or it was naturally the work of the summer sun, now growing out.

My shoulders rose up further, my arms tightly at my sides, hands deep in my pockets as my heart rate shot up from a reaction that was not fear. Mr. Gold was Mr. Gorgeous. He wasn't traditionally attractive. His nose was too long, his brow too furrowed. But there was something about the way that he'd been put together that was commanding, powerful. Just sexy. Holy shit. So good and so awful all at the same time, because I wasn't comfortable around men in general, and certainly not a good-looking one.

He scratched the beard stubble on his chin. "So where is Hattie? Are you a niece of hers or something?"

"Um…" He didn't know that Hattie had quit? Bad to worse. "I'm her replacement, sir. She's moving to Florida to live with her son."

He frowned. "Stop calling me, sir. It makes me feel grandiose. And old." He tilted his head and looked me up and down. "Though compared to you I guess I am old." His expression was amused, rueful. "Maybe even crusty."

Not the adjective I would use to describe him. I was suddenly aware of the fact that I wasn't wearing a bra, and didn't even need one. Because my shirt was too short, a large sliver of my belly was showing. I didn't know what to say, so I said nothing. Just stood there.

"I'd forgotten Hattie quit. My assistant said she hired a replacement. Am I to take it that's you?"

"Yes. Today is my first day." Hopefully not my last. I didn't like the way he was looking at me. Like he found me curious. Lacking. He clearly thought I was too young for the job. My palms started to sweat. I had zero experience being in the company of hot older guys who were rich. I didn't even have any experience with young, ugly, broke guys. I'd spent most of high school taking care of my grandmother or hanging out online when I could sneak away from her. "You have a beautiful house."

He looked around, like he was seeing it for the first time. "I suppose I do, don't I? Thanks, Tiffany. And I guess I should introduce myself. Devin Gold." He dropped his bag on the floor and held his hand out to me.

Wiping my own hand quickly on the inside of my pocket to rid my skin of clamminess, I hastily raised it and put it into his. I expected a quick, swift, nothing of a touch, but he gripped my hand firmly and held it longer than I was comfortable with.

"Nice to meet you," he said, studying me intently.

His interest wasn't sexual. I'd seen enough of that from sweaty older foster brothers. It was just an… assessment. He was a businessman after all. He had created massive success for major music stars. He obviously knew how to read people. I wondered what he saw when he looked at me.

Most likely I didn't want to know.

But the scrutiny had me raising my chin slightly. If there was one thing I knew how to do, it was maintain my pride with someone else in the power position. "It's nice to meet you, too. Sir."

He laughed softly and let go of my hand. "Come in the family room, Tiffany, and keep me company. You can tell me why a young girl wants to housesit by herself in a pretentious mini-mansion on an obscure part of the Maine coast."

And maybe he could tell me why he was there and how soon he was leaving. His presence was unnerving. Okay, it was also arousing. But that was bad. Really, really bad. I could not develop a crush on my boss. He would think I was completely ridiculous if he found out, and he'd fire me. I would have nowhere to go if I lost this cushy gig.

Slapping his hand to his thigh to call the dog, he moved into the family room. "It's dark in here. You can override the timers, you know. Just use the switches."

"I like the dark," I lied, not wanting to admit that I'd been afraid imaginary serial killers were creeping around outside checking me out.

"I like the dark too." He went over to the fireplace and opened the doors. "But I also like a fire. Can't do that at my place in Manhattan."

Sitting down on the easy chair, I busied my hands by petting the dog, who had come right over and rested his head on my knees. "What's the dog's name?"

"Amelia."

"So you're a girl," I murmured to the Lab, rubbing behind her ears.

"I like girls," Mr. Gold said, his back to me as he skillfully built a pyre from the woodpile recessed into the stone wall.

The words seemed flirty, charming. But the tone didn't. He just sounded matter-of-fact, which was way more unnerving than if he had been shamelessly flirtatious. My minimal experience with guys had been limited to boys and creepers. Plus a handful of foster fathers who had been decent men, like Cat's dad. That was it. I didn't know how to read Mr. Gold. And I couldn't bring myself to think of him as Devin. That name was too familiar, too romantic, too college student. It would be too easy to forget he was my employer if I was thinking of him as Devin. He was going to have to stay Mr. Gold while he was there.

"You're a pretty girl," I told Amelia as her earnest dark eyes stared up at me. It was much easier to talk to animals than it was to humans.

Within another minute there was a fire blazing and he stood back up, stretching. I could practically smell the manliness so I crossed my legs. Tightly. It was a suck ass time for my hormones to decide to stand at attention. But there was something intriguing about him and as he moved past the coffee table he gave a nod to the open doughnut box.

"I see someone likes those almost as much as me. Though I find it hard to believe someone as tiny as you could pack away three in one day."

"I don't think you're supposed to point out when a woman overeats," I said, without thinking, mortified to have been busted. Hey, I like fried dough. Who didn't?

That drew him up short, his hand pausing as he reached out for a doughnut. "Fair enough. My apologies. One of the downsides of being rich is that no one dares to reprimand me."

Oh, God, he thought I'd reprimanded him? Well, I had, but clearly I'd been too blunt. It was a bad habit. I hastened to correct my mistake. "I wasn't saying you were wrong. I was just joking. But I have terrible delivery. I don't sound funny. Do I?"

"No. You don't." He lifted the doughnut. "But no worries. I wasn't upset. In fact, I liked that you were being honest, so don't pretend you were joking."

He was right. I hadn't been joking. I appreciated that he recognized that.

He took a bite of the pastry and chewed, his eyes closing briefly. "Glorious. I'm going to open a bottle of wine. Do you want a glass?"

That had to be a trick question. I shook my head hastily. "No."

"I can hear you thinking," he said, shaking the doughnut in my direction. "You're worried that you're underage and what does it mean that I just offered you wine, aren't you?"

Yes.

"Maybe that I'm trying to bait you into doing something illegal and then call you out for it, or maybe that I'm a pervert and I'm trying to get you drunk." He gave a little smile. "Trust me, it wasn't either. Just that it felt rude to not offer you some."

It seemed to me that maybe he could have offered me a soft

drink. But what did I know? It wasn't that often anyone offered me anything at all, unless it was a criticism. "I'm fine."

"You're tense. You're looking at me like I'm a big bad wolf." He cocked his head. "I have to say it's not a reaction I get nearly as often as I should."

That was puzzling enough that I spoke before I thought about the consequences. "You want people to be afraid of you?"

"No, of course not. I just want people to stop kissing my ass. Stop lying to me."

I had to guess that suck ups were a huge part of a rich guy's reality. While it didn't sound fun, you were still rich. So that right there exempted you from a certain percentage of pity parties. In my opinion. "No one ever lies to me," I told him. "Sometimes it would be nice if they did."

An *I love you* from my gram would have gone a long way.

"So you be honest with me and I'll lie to you, how does that sound?"

I shook my head. "You don't know the right things to lie to me about. So because I know you don't know, I will think everything you're saying is a lie, or I'll wonder if it's a lie, and then I'll never know what to think."

He let out a rusty laugh, before walking to the kitchen. His chuckles followed me. "Very good point, Tiffany," he called over his shoulder. "Let's try a policy of mutual honesty with each other then. And when you have my measure, you can ask me to start lying. Or maybe clue me in on what you'd like me to lie about and we can start now."

Turning in my chair, I watched him bend over and open the wine fridge. His jeans pulled across his ass. I had never seen a butt like that off the Internet or apart from underwear ads in the *Cosmo* magazines I read at the public library. This was a man who had hired a personal trainer. If I had the option of choosing what he should lie to me about, I could spin a fantasy pretty damn quick involving him telling me I was beautiful. I had a great imagination. Growing up it was all I'd owned.

He stood up, catching me staring at him. "No?"

I shook my head. "There wouldn't be any satisfaction in that."

"And the ultimate goal is always personal satisfaction, isn't it?"

"That seems to be the general consensus," I said, without hesitation.

He deftly uncorked the bottle. "You're an odd little creature. So serious. You've lived on Vinalhaven your whole life?"

Feeling insulted, I frowned. "Yes."

"And your family?"

"What about them?"

"Mom and dad, happily married? Three younger siblings?"

I shook my head. Stick to the facts and hope he didn't pry. "I never met my father. Mother ran off when I was two. I was mostly in foster care, and sometimes with my grandmother."

For a second he didn't say anything, frowning as he filled his glass. Then he came toward me, taking a sip of wine as he strolled. "I'm sorry. Family doesn't always live up to our expectations."

Most people didn't live up to my expectations. At a certain point you stopped having them. "YOLO," I told him, going for flippant, because I felt the familiar stain of shame that I was the poor social services girl. "Make the best of it, right?"

He sat down on the couch and when I expected him to sink

back into it, master of his home, he actually set his glass on the coffee table and leaned forward, forearms on his knees. "Don't go Valley Girl on me, I'm begging you. If you say you're going to take a selfie I guarantee I will stab myself in the face. No. Just no. I hate it on anyone, but even more on you because you don't mean it."

The conviction with which he spoke had me raising my eyebrows. "I should have read the job description more carefully." Then because I couldn't resist, I added, "Note to self: No selfies."

The corner of his mouth turned up, and he relaxed back against the cushions. "Your delivery definitely isn't funny, but you are. Welcome to Richfield, Tiffany." He raised his glass in salute. "Where the truth sets you free."

Now it was my turn to smile, before I could stop myself. I tried to dial it back, but I was too incredulous to prevent my mouth was splitting, even as I wanted to wipe it away.

"What?" he asked, pausing as he reached for his glass.

"That's such a lie," I told him.

Mr. Gold smiled. "Truth." He popped the second half of his doughnut in his mouth.

Amelia had burrowed her head further between my legs and I stroked behind her ears. "You're so sweet," I murmured to her, more comfortable looking down at her than at my employer.

"If she's bothering you just push her away."

Hadn't I just said she was sweet? It didn't make sense to me that he would suggest I found it annoying. "No, she's fine." I wasn't going to push anyone away who sought affection from me. I'd been on the receiving end of that shove too often. "I've never had a dog." Again and again I stroked my hands down her head, behind the ears, and along her back, her satin fur allowing an easy glide of my touch down her flank. "She's so calm."

He didn't say anything and I looked up at him, realizing that I'd been thinking out loud, wondering if I should just excuse myself and go to my room. He probably wanted to be alone in his own house, not entertaining the housesitter. Why was he there, at the house he didn't like, anyway? When I caught his eye what I saw made me hitch my breath. He was watching me with an intensity that I didn't understand, but that had my hand stilling on Amelia, my body tingling in places it had no right to tingle. I wanted desperately to ask him why he was at the house and how long he was going to stay, but if there was one thing I knew, it was that my role was never to ask questions.

I recognized that was why I was so nosy online, why I had learned to poke and sift through the Internet and find out anything I was curious about. Because face to face with people, I wasn't supposed to ask questions. It wasn't my role, and it was hard to stay so obedient, so detached. I also knew the minute I went into my room, I was going to Google the shit out of Devin Gold and see what I could find beyond the obvious that I already knew, which was that he owned the house and he was hot.

"Would you mind if I left Amelia here with you when I go back?" he asked. "She is so much happier here than in the city, and I think it would make me feel better about you being here by yourself."

"I can take care of myself," I said, defensively. It was a knee-jerk reaction, even though I knew I would love to have the dog with me. But I didn't want it to sound like I needed the dog. I didn't need anything or anyone, and I wanted him to understand that.

"No doubt," he said, nodding, his tone clearly indicating he didn't believe it for one second. "I'm sure if attacked by a desperate meth-head twice your size, you'd be perfectly capable of defending yourself."

"I thought that's why there's a security system. And how many meth-heads are running around the coast?" It was stupid logic. "Hattie didn't have a dog."

"Hattie would bake a burglar cookies and they would part ways the best of friends. Are you saying you don't want the dog?"

Both my hands came out instinctively to cover Amelia's ears, like she could understand what he was saying. "What, no! That's not what I'm saying. But I don't want to steal your dog. You shouldn't leave her because you're worried about me. I'll be fine."

"It's not stealing if it's my idea," he said wryly. "And it would be better for Amelia, truly."

How could I resist those eyes? And I didn't mean the dog's. He was giving me a very sincere look, his eyes a curious amber color with gold flecks. They were mesmerizing, and the fact that he might actually have any sort of concern for my safety made me feel shy, uncomfortable. "Okay, sir, thank you."

He shook his head with a sound of exasperation. "What is your last name, Tiffany?"

The random question threw me. I answered obediently. "Ennis."

"Have a doughnut, Miss Ennis." He lifted the box and held it in my direction.

So my continued use of "sir" had him using my last name. The only time I was called Miss Ennis was in court by judges deciding my fate. It left a sour taste in my mouth, but it wasn't his fault, so I said nothing. I just reached out and took one of the doughnuts he was offering and tore into the sugary sweetness with my teeth. "Thank you," I muttered around the mouthful.

"You're welcome." He drained his wine glass. "So what do you think of my house? Do you really think it's beautiful?"

"Yes. It's very big," I said, chewing so I could swallow. I was going to elaborate, but the food stuck in my throat.

"It is that. It's a lot of things, and truthfully I like Maine more than I like this house. I appreciate the space, the view." He plucked at a throw pillow. "But I don't get out here as much as I used to. I really should come more."

No. No, he shouldn't. I said nothing. Just chewed.

I had been hoping for peace and quiet. Craving it. If Devin Gold was in residence I wasn't going to get either.

"I'm planning to stay a week."

Jesus. That was about six days longer than I wanted. "I guess it was kind of bad timing for me to start this job. Do you want me to go stay somewhere else?" Cat would take me back. There was no ferry to Vinalhaven after five, but I could take one in the morning.

"Is that what you think I would do? Send you away on your first day?"

That definitely was a trick question. "I think it's normal that you'd want to be alone in your house."

"Don't make assumptions about me, Miss Ennis."

I felt the burn start on my cheeks and spread across my face. Yet my pride couldn't allow the apology to pass my lips. I hadn't done anything wrong. I hadn't done anything wrong at all.

He was going to fire me. I was going to lose this job on the first day. But I couldn't say anything. I just sat there, tense, refusing to drop my gaze, refusing to blink.

"I'm going to take a shower," he announced, standing up. "I guess I wasted a fire." He pushed the logs over with the poker and tossed ashes from the bottom over it, tamping out the flames. Standing again, he called to the dog, "Come on, Amelia. I'll let you sleep on my bed tonight."

His dog turned her head to look at him, but she didn't move. He made a sound of annoyance in the back of his throat. "Really?"

I nudged her with my knees. "Go on. Go with your dad." That reminded me of the stupid nickname I'd read online about him. Gold Daddy. It so didn't suit him. The man I was seeing didn't seem like a swanky player. But it was probably a public persona, an image thing.

Amelia stayed put. "Sorry," I said, embarrassed.

But he just shrugged. "She'll sleep with anyone. Seems to be a common problem with women in my life."

Was he saying someone had cheated on him? That seemed… insane. Who would screw around if they were sharing a bed with him?

But I'd never shared a bed with anyone romantically so I wasn't exactly going on any concrete experience. "It's probably because I'm new. She's curious."

"Again, a problem with the women in my life." He smiled, but it wasn't pleasant or kind. "Good night, Tiffany. Make yourself at home. I mean that."

That was the last thing in the world I wanted to do. Home wasn't a place I ever wanted to return. "Good night, Mr. Gold.

Thank you." I wanted to say something about how I was grateful, I appreciated the opportunity, but every wording I thought up sounded stupid or pathetic or too ass kissing, so I defaulted to silence. You could never say the wrong thing if you said nothing at all.

"I'm not at work. Call me Devin. Please."

He looked so earnest, I nodded, even though I knew I'd never say it out loud.

If he was leaving the family room, I felt like I should too, so I stood up, forcing Amelia to lift her head. She looked up at me. "What?" I asked the dog. I wasn't versed in pet communication.

"She's just waiting for you." Devin had kicked off his shoes at some point and was standing by the foyer, clearly intending to head up the grand staircase. I knew the master bedroom was upstairs, but since I'd been in the house less than a day, I had yet to see it. His hair was in his eyes and he didn't bother to push it away, and his expression was neutral, unreadable.

"Where does she think I'm going?"

"To bed."

"Oh, well, I am." I took a step, leaning over to flip the lid closed on the doughnut box.

Amelia trotted towards Devin, then stopped and looked back at me.

"My room is this way," I told her, pointing toward the kitchen. It should have felt stupid having a one-sided conversation with a dog, but it was way easier to talk to her than it was to Devin Gold.

I was afraid if I looked at him, he would read too much on my face. How vulnerable I felt, despite my desperate conviction and desire to be independent.

"She's expecting us to go to bed together."

My gaze snapped up from the dog to him, palms instantly sweating. My eyes widened, I couldn't help it. He wasn't flirting. He wasn't being suggestive. He was just stating a fact that the dog would expect her master to have a woman with him. It had nothing to do with me.

There must be a lot of women ready and willing to share his bed.

Heat bloomed on my cheeks and I was grateful for the dark room so he couldn't see my embarrassment. My sudden desire. My awkward reaction.

"I guess she'll have to choose then. She'll pick you." I was confident she would.

So when I started walking in the opposite direction I was surprised to hear toenails clicking on the hardwood floors and dog tags jingling. A glance back showed Amelia crossing the room to me. "Oh!"

He gave me a mocking salute. "I relinquish my traitorous dog to you. Though I do tend to kick her by accident, so I'm sure it's partly that and partly that she has good taste in companions."

Before I could absorb the compliment, he added, "She always hated my ex-wife, go figure."

"Did you kick her too?" It was out before I could stop it.

But Devin gave me a sly smile. "Just to the curb." Then he retrieved his bag off the floor and sauntered up the stairs, raising his arm in a casual wave. "Good night."

"Good night." I fast walked to my room, trembling hands jammed in my pockets.

In my new room I shut the door behind me, locked it, and

flicked on the light. Amelia jumped on my bed.

I promptly pulled out my ancient iPad I'd bought for a steal and started seeing what I could find out about Gold Daddy.

And who exactly he had been married to.

Shucking my jeans, I slid beneath the covers, onto crisp, cool sheets. They felt amazing and expensive as they caressed my skin. As I pulled up an image of Devin on my iPad, I spontaneously yanked my tank top over my head and rocked a little under the comforter, sighing at the luxurious sensation of clean and quality sheets next to my near nudity.

"Oh, God," I breathed, when I saw Devin onscreen dressed in a tux and sunglasses. So damn sexy. So damn rich. It was astonishing to see him there on a gossip news website, leaving the Grammys, a cocky grin on his face, and to know that he was upstairs in bed. Right above me.

Real.

Did he sleep naked? In his underwear? I'd never been so close to either a rich guy or a good-looking guy. It was overwhelming, exciting. I wouldn't have thought I'd be star struck, and I wasn't. Not exactly. It was more surreal than anything else. Like before now the world on my computer screen wasn't real. Those people didn't exist outside the box of the Internet. Yet they did. He did.

And he liked doughnuts and studied me with an unnerving intensity.

Staring at his smile onscreen, wishing I could see behind the sunglasses, I shifted my legs restlessly. I was turned on, I couldn't help myself. The sheets were cool, the privacy compelling, the image of the man delicious. Tentatively, I slipped my fingers down between my thighs and stroked myself to a hot, wet arousal. The more I thought about Devin upstairs, the more I relaxed, and let myself enjoy the intimate contours of my body, my underutilized sexual desires clamoring for escape.

Conscious of having Amelia as an audience, I kept the covers up to my chin, my breathing even. I was used to being quiet.

When I came, my eyes were closed and I was imagining him over me, his lips pressing hot kisses on my sensitive flesh. As the tremors of ecstasy slowed, I turned my head to look at him again.

My screen had gone dark.

And suddenly I felt more alone than ever before.

chapter three

FINGERING THE NOTE ON THE kitchen island, I stared down at Devin's bold handwriting.

Got called back to NYC. Text me if Amelia is a problem.

He'd left his number then signed it "DG."

Next to the note was the dog's leash and instructions on how much to feed her. Behind that was the box of doughnuts with "Finish these" written on the box.

I had come into the kitchen fully dressed, nervous to see him, yet undeniably excited. To find the note was deflating. My first thought was somehow he had known, sensed, that I thought he was hot and it made him uncomfortable. Like somehow he knew that I had been lying in bed, touching myself to thoughts of him. In his house. On his sheets.

So mortifying.

Not that he knew. He couldn't know. But in the morning

light, I still felt totally self-conscious and ridiculous.

I had dressed in jeans, a sweatshirt, and my Converse, and I took the leash off the counter, determined to take the dog for a walk and stop acting and feeling like an idiot. It was better this way. I did not need Devin Gold hanging around inadvertently fostering my socially awkward crush.

"Come on, Amelia," I said, bending over and clipping the leash to her collar. I couldn't believe that Devin had entrusted me with his dog. I had never owned a pet and I had given myself a ten minute online crash course on the Labrador breed and their needs first thing when I'd woken up. It was second nature to me to reach for my iPad and do research about anything and everything. It had been my lifeline to the outside world for years, and I figured I knew a little bit about a lot of things. Jack of all trades, master of nothing.

I had wandered online for hours every day, but had never done much of anything. My life experience was nonexistent. Unless you considered using a box of Clairol to dye an old lady's hair a life experience.

As I took the dog and we walked across the yard, down towards the ocean, I wondered what New York City was really like. I'd seen it in a million movies and TV shows, had read about it online, but what would it be like to be standing in Times Square? What did it smell like? Would I feel less singled out, less obvious, less the biracial abandoned foster girl in a city where there was every color and kind of human being in existence?

It wasn't likely I'd find out anytime soon.

But my research had shown that Devin owned not just the house I was staying in, but an apartment in Manhattan on the

live for *me*

Upper East Side. He'd paid 3.3 million for the three bedroom pre-war apartment four years earlier. He had also married Kadence Creed a year after that, the daughter of his mentor, Owen Creed, a legendary music producer. According to TMZ they had split up six months earlier after a trip to Mexico for Devin's thirtieth birthday. I figured three years was the average life span of an entertainment industry marriage.

Like milk, they soured quickly.

As we walked, or more accurately, Amelia dragged me over the brown grass, I pulled my phone out of my pocket and quickly found the picture I'd discovered the night before of Kadence and Devin at their wedding. It was a Vegas ceremony and she was wearing a short dress, her boobs bursting out of the top. She looked like she had strolled out of the Playboy mansion and right on down the aisle. Big hair. Big acrylic nails. Big eyelashes. Everything was large and fake and exaggerated.

It grossed me out that this was the type of chick he would go for. But for all I knew, maybe she was super sweet. Maybe she cooked dinner for him and thoughtfully walked the dog and laughed at all his jokes. Somehow I doubted it.

I was being judgmental because I thought not only was he good looking, he was interesting. And I was jealous. Just flat out, plain old, pointlessly jealous. Kadence had money and success. An exciting life.

I had five bucks, no family, exactly two friends, and a future that stretched ahead of me as an endless struggle to survive. Yesterday I had arrived at Richfield full of hope, appreciative of the beautiful place to stay, the decent income I could stash away to hopefully start online college classes, grateful for the quiet.

34

Ready to be left alone.

Now I was alone.

And somehow Devin had tainted that, made it not good enough.

I also hated to see that it was true- that women who primped themselves into living Barbies got the guy. You never saw a rich dude with a librarian.

Or a short girl from Vinalhaven.

It made me angry.

Fuck him. Screw him and his designer sunglasses and his ridiculous need to have a box of doughnuts available to him at all times. Because clearly being denied anything when you wanted it was a foreign concept to Gold Daddy. Big pimpin', take his coin, and buy the world, yo. Fucking tool.

Leaning down, I picked up a rock and hurled it off the cliff with all my strength. It fell so far to the water below that I never even saw the splash.

My phone rang in my hand. It was Cat.

"Hey," I said, breathless, but wanting someone to talk to.

"Hey! How goes the housesitting? Is it like insanely beautiful there?"

"Yes. The house is amazeballs." I always cranked up the teen speak with Cat because it drove her crazy. She thought it made me sound cliché.

If you say you're going to take a selfie I'll stab myself.

Yeah. He popped right back into my head.

"I'm so jealous. Heath is outside chopping wood right now because this house is so damn drafty. I can never get warm. I bet you can crank the heat up and he'll never even notice. You'll be living in a sauna all winter. Your skin will glow like a Neutrogena commercial."

Sitting down on the hard ground, I let Amelia lick my hand. It tickled, but there was something about having a connection with another living creature that was awesome. I could see the appeal of having a pet. The dog was great company, a silent and constant companion through the night and that morning. "The heat is on a timer. It's all controlled electronically through software. So he can basically control the heat in the house from his offices in New York City."

The tech geek in me loved that. But it also suddenly occurred to me that if the house was wired that way, most likely there were cameras monitoring the property. Was I living in the Big Brother house? Didn't they have to disclose that to me? Though I wasn't sure who the mysterious "they" was. But again I remembered the night before with pure horror. Even if they couldn't tell what I was doing under the covers, I was still staring endlessly at Devin's image on my computer screen.

Holy shit.

Somewhere in some glass tower in New York was a team of his employees smirking over me? Watching me lie in bed researching Devin. Watching me eat a doughnut this morning that I totally didn't need in two offensive and gooey bites.

"That sucks."

"Do you think the house could be monitored by cameras?" I asked Cat. "Is it illegal for them to do that without telling me?"

"I have no idea. I mean, it's his private property. But if he had cameras sweeping the house, why would he need you there?"

Good point. "Squatters? He and his assistant seem weirdly

convinced drug addicts will break into any empty house and start cooking meth."

"That must be a New York thing. But if the cameras showed someone breaking in, the security system would alert the cops and they would come. You totally wouldn't need to be living there if he had that much technology rolling."

"I don't think my job is to keep it safe from an invasion. I think it's to make sure that when he is feeling random and wants to show up whenever it won't be dusty and he'll have food to eat. I have a list of stuff I have to keep stocked in the pantry at all times and let me tell you, the dude likes wine and sugar."

"A man after my own heart."

I took a deep breath and confessed. "He showed up here last night."

"What? On your first night? That seems creeper. Are you okay? What's he like?"

That was a more loaded question than she could ever imagine. The ground was making my ass numb. I stood up and brushed at the seat of my jeans. "He's not what I was expecting. He looks like a model for a cologne ad. Rugged and sexy. He came with his dog, drank a glass of wine, ate a doughnut, built a fire, slept here, then left this morning."

"Rich people are freaks. Why did he come all the way from New York for like a twelve-hour stay?"

"He said he got called back to the city, whatever that means."

"He didn't hit on you, did he?"

Amelia was tugging hard on the leash, so I started walking again. "Cat, I love you, but you need to stop with this idea that there are actually men hitting on me. It doesn't happen. Ever."

"You're just blind to it. You're so used to tuning out criticism, you tune out compliments too without realizing it."

And she was biased. That was all there was to it. "He did not hit on me. His ex-wife looks like one of the real housewives. I don't think I'm his type, so you can rest assured my hymen isn't in jeopardy."

"Don't joke about that. I worry about you."

Sometimes you just had to laugh, or you would sob. "I'm fine. I'm living in a big ass house with a fully stocked fridge. I have a queen bed and I've never seen so many scented candles in my life. I'm better than fine. I'm awesome, actually."

I was. Fuck Devin Gold and his amber eyes that made me feel inadequate. Fuck my insecurities and my fears.

"Hold on. I'm getting a text."

I pulled my phone out and touched the screen to read the text from a number I didn't have saved in my contacts.

Just an FYI, not returning to Richfield this week. Probably won't be back until December.

Obviously Mr. Gold. Who also obviously assumed I had immediately saved his number in my phone since he didn't say who he was in the text.

Another text buzzed. *If A is a problem let me know. I can come back for her.*

"Let me call you back," I told Cat, after putting the phone up to my ear. "It's the master of the manor texting me."

She made a snorting sound. "Nice. Okay, call me later. And send me pictures of his house."

"No!"

"I'm not going to post them online. I just want to see the

inside."

"You can just come over, you know."

"Are you allowed to have people over?"

Now that she mentioned it, I had no idea. "Let me get back to you on that."

After I hung up with Cat, I stood on the hard-packed dirt and let the wind pummel me. It smelled like rain was coming and the gusts made me wish I had kept my hair short instead of growing it out of sheer boredom. The strands were repeatedly getting tangled in my eyelashes and sticking to my lips. My fingers were starting to numb from the cold but I didn't want to go back to the house yet.

I texted Devin back.

K. A is fine with me. Am I allowed to have friends over?

After saving his number as Gold Daddy I started to tuck the phone away, assuming it would be awhile before he got back to me. I was startled when it buzzed immediately in my hand.

Like a boyfriend?

No. My foster sister and her boyfriend. To hang out.

That's fine. No overnight guests.

So what, he didn't want me having sex in his house? Like I would ever even contemplate that. If I were having sex with anyone. Which I wasn't. And never had.

Well, aside from myself.

God. I had to really figure out how to ask if there were cameras in the house. But if I did, he would assume I was intending to do something I wasn't supposed to.

K, thanks.

Make sure you lock up and don't walk around alone at night.

Was this what it felt like to have a father? The last thing I wanted was for him to go all paternal on me. Not when I was pretty sure I could orgasm just by looking at him. Weird. It was all just weird.

Yes, sir.

He sent me a face with its eyes rolling in exasperation.

I laughed, all alone on the coast, without another human being in sight.

My phone rang, indicating an actual call. Gold Daddy. The name so didn't suit him. Not to me anyway.

"Hello?" I said, suddenly nervous.

"Hey, it's Devin." There was a rustling as he adjusted his phone.

What, like now he was going to announce himself? "Hi." I waited for him to explain why he was calling. I could hear voices in the background.

"Yes, the ahi tuna," he said. "Thank you."

He was ordering dinner. I kept waiting, suddenly annoyed. I didn't want to be multi-tasked.

"Tuna is ick," a female voice said, loudly enough that I could hear the words clearly, register her horror. I wondered if he had me on speaker phone.

"No one said you had to eat it," Devin said mildly. "Tiffany?"

Right there. Waiting patiently. It's what I did. "Yes."

"I just wanted to let you know that you can take Amelia off her leash. She'll come back to you if you call for her."

"Okay." He could have texted that to me.

"Who are you talking to?" the female voice whined. "God, it's like every two seconds you're on the phone."

"It's business, sweetheart. Daddy has to pay the bills."

I just about threw up in my mouth. Could he sound more patronizing? Could she sound more bratty and stupid?

"This wind sucks, it ruined my hair. Though I mean, I am lucky I can usually work the windswept look," unknown woman said.

Nice complain-a-brag. She'd done that like a pro. I had zero problem picturing the woman he was with-tall, blonde, tan.

"Most of us did get the short end of the genetic stick compared to you," he told her.

How could he foster that arrogance? How could he not be annoyed with her? She was as ick as ahi tuna. I made faces at Amelia, and stabbing gestures towards the phone.

"Now let me talk for a second, Brooke. Stop pouting and show me your pretty smile."

I couldn't help it. I gave an involuntary snort. He didn't even sound like the same man who'd been in the house with me the night before. This guy sounded like the type of dude I had pictured originally. A sunglass-wearing plastic surgery victim with a bevy of inappropriately young chicks on both arms. My lip curled up in disgust.

But Devin heard me. "Is there something you'd like to say, Tiffany?"

I stared back at the house. Its grandeur dominated the coastline. "No." Then because I couldn't resist, I added, "You called me."

"I did. Maybe because in the midst of my ridiculous life I wanted to talk to someone normal. It doesn't matter."

Was I normal? His life ridiculous? I supposed both were true.

He definitely had me on speaker. I could hear the woman quite clearly now, like she'd moved in very close to him. "Why did I wear this dress, G Daddy, if you're not even going to look at me?"

"Then let's go take it off you," he said brusquely.

Wow. The shock of his harsh words hit me, my cold fingers slipping on my phone. "I should let you go," I managed to blurt out. "Is there something specific you wanted? Are you coming back to Richfield?"

There was a pause. "No. I'm not coming back."

I should have been relieved. Yet I was disappointed. He was a puzzle I couldn't sort out. The only bit of excitement in an otherwise extremely dull life. "If you change your mind, the doughnuts are here, waiting."

"You make me feel like a pretentious asshole." The "s" is asshole slurred.

It finally dawned on me that he was drunk. That would explain the random phone call, the weird comments. "I don't make you feel anything. You do that to yourself."

He gave a muffled laugh. "I'm glad I left the dog with you. You look so small on the security camera, walking around outside."

I swallowed hard. So he could see me, at least on the exterior of the house. "I'm fine."

"I hope so. I find myself worrying about you."

"That's nice of you." Weird. But nice.

"Sometimes I am nice. And sometimes I'm brutally selfish."

"That doesn't make you unique." Then because it was a conversation that couldn't really go anywhere but weirder still, I added, "I should let you go. I think your friend wants you to herself."

"Yeah. What do *you* want, Tiffany?"

I closed my eyes, longing rising in me without warning. I wanted to be loved. Cherished. Cared for. I wanted to matter to someone, anyone. I wanted a guy to look at me and not see what he could get from me, but what he could give to me. Friendship. Companionship. Partnership.

"I want to be alone," I told him, finally, voice quiet. Firm.

There was truth to it. It just wasn't the whole truth.

"Then you're in the right place."

Opening my eyes again, I watched the wind kick up the waves in the water, big angry bursts of ombre color- black to navy to aqua to white. With the nearest neighbors a half mile down the road, I could fall into the ocean and no one would notice. I could disappear and it would be days before anyone thought to wonder what had happened to me.

Yet for the first time, I was master of my own destiny. No one cared what happened to me, but I did. Here, at Richfield, I could be myself, figure out my future.

"Yeah," I told him. "You're right. I am in the right place."

When I went back inside I decided to give in to my curiosity and explore the house. Ignoring the formal rooms on the first floor I had already glanced in, I went up the stairs, opening bedroom after bedroom door. None were particularly unique or interesting. Just lots of traditional furnishings that matched the New England vibe of the house. The dark wood didn't look like something that Devin's ex-wife would choose, but neither did it look like his style. Not that I knew either one of them, but if I had a house, I would think my furniture would reflect my personal style.

Not that I had much style at present, but I'd want a colorful, casual house. Warm. Playful.

In what was most likely the master bedroom, I drew up short in the doorway. There was a doll on the bed. Just sitting there, in the middle of the mountain of pillows. Not an antique doll, but a modern one, styled in a short pink skirt and tight sweater, blonde hair. Amelia had fallen asleep in front of the fireplace so I was exploring alone and after glancing behind me like I might get busted by an invisible person, I took a tentative step forward. Unless Devin had a daughter or a niece I didn't know about, that doll was creepy as hell.

Picking it up, I brushed the hair back and studied the face. It looked familiar and I figured it had to be some pop culture reference I wasn't connecting the dots to. I had never owned a doll myself. But then I took a peek at the inside of the sweater and saw the tag was a designer label. Whether real or not, I had no idea. Below that it said, "Special Edition Kadence Doll."

OMG, it was a fucking doll of his ex-wife. I set it back down, horrified, and whirled around. Movement behind me made me jump until I realized I was just seeing my own reflection in the giant mirror over the dresser.

"Jesus," I whispered, putting my hand on my chest to steady my breathing. I looked pale, dark eyes huge as they stared back at me. I had pulled my black hair back off my face, but a few wisps had escaped on top, giving me a disheveled look.

And to think for half a second, I'd actually fantasized that maybe Devin Gold found me interesting in an intellectual sort of way.

Maybe some day there would be a guy for me, but it wouldn't be Rich Dude who dated supermodels and kept a fugly weird-ass doll of his ex-wife on his bed.

For that, I should be grateful.

Yet that didn't stop me from checking my phone to see if I had missed a call from him or if he had texted.

I hadn't. He didn't

chapter
four

*J*AMMING A TOOTHPICK INTO A cupcake, I bent over the oven in Devin's kitchen and carefully assessed the results. Clean. Cupcakes done. Satisfied, I pulled them out with oven mitts and set them to cool. Baking was my new thing, especially at night when the darkness pressed in on me.

Actually, a lot of things were my new things. It had been six weeks since I had moved into Richfield and its blissful silence, and quiet luxury. I had filled my days with dusting, cooking, taking ridiculously long showers, and reading dozens of ebooks. I rode to town on my bike and got groceries and checked out tapes on learning French from the local library. As I started cleaning up the mixing bowl and measuring cups, French filled the room from the DVD I had inserted into the laptop that sat on the desk in the kitchen.

Verbs. Etre. Aller. Avoir.

I liked the rhythm of the language. I didn't think I was actually learning a damn word, but it filled the house with sound. It was the one thing I had expected to love about living alone, the lack of noise. And I did. But it also echoed around me, foreign and profound. So I almost always had music or the TV on.

As for the mental solitude, hell, I was used to that. Gram hadn't been good company. She had never once asked me how I was or for my opinion. Being away from her just allowed me the ability to indulge in doing whatever I wanted, whenever I wanted. It rocked. I was pretty sure that I couldn't be any happier, ever. I knew I was going to have to stick to my plan to save my money and start nursing school the following year, but for now, I was content to roll through each easy day. This was my version of spring break. A party of privacy.

It wasn't my house, but considering I was the only person ever in it, I had settled in, and felt comfortable there. I never heard from Devin. The owner, as I forced myself to think of him. Hadn't since the day I'd woken up to find him gone and he had said that he wouldn't be back until December. I wasn't sure what that meant, exactly, if he was planning a big holiday or whatever at Richfield, but it was still two weeks away so I still had time before he interrupted my routine.

I had mixed feelings about that. I wanted to see him, because he intrigued me, but I knew he was going to make me feel ridiculous.

As I went to the pantry for the container of frosting I had bought, my phone chimed with a Google alert.

So, okay, I was stalking Devin online. I couldn't help it. It was too easy, and I got a sick thrill at the voyeurism of seeing what he was doing in New York while I stayed in his country house. Over the past month, the only mentions had been a new record deal for one of his clients and two pictures of him with a leggy blonde underwear model at fashion week. The kind of woman I would expect him to be with, and while it had made me feel about as attractive as a stubby little garden gnome, I had to begrudgingly admit her appearance was an improvement over his ex-wife. This woman didn't look quite so fake. Just thin, chic, and gorgeous.

This alert was a pic of them together from a gossip magazine's website under the header "Fall Beach bodies." He wasn't the focus, she was. Brooke. And her amazing bikini body as she splashed Devin in the water.

So the blonde was the whiner who didn't like ahi tuna and wanted "Daddy's" full attention.

"On vacay in Turks and Caicos, Brooke shows off her incredible abs," I read out loud. "Can you believe that, Amelia?" I asked the dog, who didn't even blink from her curled-up position in her dog bed. It sat next to the island, and the fabric matched the stool cushions. "How does this stuff get published? Who cares?"

The answer was, of course, me. Not about the identity of Brooke's trainer but about the fact that Devin was in the shot, looking pissed off at her. That was not a man who was frolicking. Though it was a man who himself had a great body below that stormy expression. I eyeballed his chest longer than I should have. "How is it some people are rich *and* good looking? What's up with that? Spread it around, God."

Amelia suddenly raised her head and listened. Not to my pointless babbling, but to a noise at the front of the house. I heard it too, though I wasn't sure what I heard.

"J'ai, tu as, il a, nous avons, vous avez," the woman's voice droned on and I walked over and hit the pause button so I could hear better.

Nothing. The house creaked, the wind blowing, but it was the usual sounds of settling.

I was just starting to relax again when the peal of the doorbell rang through the house. I jumped. "Holy crap." I'd never even heard the doorbell before. No one had come to the door in six weeks and while it wasn't super late, it was still eight o'clock and dark out. Richfield wasn't on the way to anything so it couldn't be someone lost or broken down.

Moving down the hallway gingerly, the dog trotting beside me, I slid to the side of the front window and peeked out into the dark. There was a delivery truck in the drive, firing up loudly before pulling away. My heart rate settled down. "God, Tiffany, get a grip. It's a package."

But I still found myself slowly pulling the door open and scanning the area before snatching the legal-size envelope off the front step. Not even a package, just some paperwork, clearly. I shut the door quickly behind me and flipped the dead bolt. Back in the kitchen, I hit play again for the French lesson and stared at the envelope addressed to Devin. Marked Express Urgent, it looked important. I decided to text him to ask him what I should do with it. Maybe it was something he needed right away.

He answered with a brusque *Open it.*

Wrinkling my nose, I started to pull the tab. I didn't want to see something personal or his bank statements or something. I was pretty sure the shock of his wealth in black and white would freak me the fuck out.

But it wasn't bank statements. It was a pile of pictures. Of him. Which might have seemed somewhat normal, except someone had written all over them with a Sharpie. *Liar. Cheater. Manwhore. Asshole.*

"What the hell?" I murmured, shuffling through the stack. There was one of his sports car, and the license plate had been changed to read ET PUSSY. Everything about it was venomous and just a little bit crazy. Some of the shots seemed to be candids, like he knew the person taking the picture, others were magazine clippings or clearly printed off from online. As I moved through them, suddenly they were no longer pictures of him, but of women. Brooke, the bikini babe. A tiny brunette. A tall black girl with curls I was jealous of. Another blonde. Then me. It was a picture of me, walking outside with Amelia.

WTF. I dropped it like it was hot.

My phone buzzed. *What is it?*

With trembling hands, I typed. *Pics of you and women.*

That's it?

Yes.

Just toss them.

That was it? He wasn't bothered or creeped out? Of course I hadn't told him about the slurs. I was debating if I should when the front door opened with a squeak. My stomach dropped and I turned to the dog and gestured for her to come with me. I was planning to go into my room, lock the door, and call the cops. But Amelia wouldn't come with me. She had started down the hallway, tail wagging.

"Amelia, come," I hissed in a desperate whisper. There was

an intruder in the house and the dog was going to greet him. Fabulous.

But then I realized that I had locked the front door. No one could have jimmied the deadbolt. Only a key would open the door.

"Hey, girl," a familiar masculine voice said. "You glad to see me? Yes, I missed you too." Then, "Alright, get down."

Devin.

In the house.

I loosened my death grip on my cell phone and started towards him, relieved and horrified all at once. I was wearing yoga pants and a T-shirt that had an explosion of flour down the front. It was likely I hadn't brushed my hair that day. Maybe even the day before. Crossing my arms over my chest I paused in the doorway of the kitchen to watch him.

"Hi," I said when he looked up at me.

"Hello, Tiffany." He was wearing a leather jacket, and after giving Amelia's head a final rub, he stood up and assessed me. "What?"

I shook my head.

"No, I recognize that look. It's accusing. You're mad at me for not telling you I was coming."

Yes. "Of course not. It's your house."

The corner of his mouth turned up. "Yes, it's my house, but you're still annoyed with me. I can see it all over your face. You're too honest to be a poker player, for future reference." He moved closer to me and sniffed the air. "What's that smell?"

"I made cupcakes."

His eyebrows shot up. "No shit. Can I have one?"

What, like I was going to tell him no? "Of course, Mr. Gold."

"Oh, I'm Mr. Gold again, am I? You really are annoyed with me." Though he didn't sound busted up over that fact.

"Why didn't you mention you were almost here when I just texted you?" I couldn't help it. I had to ask. I'd almost had a freaking heart attack when I'd heard the door open. "You scared me." Even I could hear the reprimand in my voice and I mentally winced. He was my boss, damn it. I needed to watch what I said.

"I'm sorry." He gave me a charming smile. "It was a last minute thing." Then without warning his finger came out and brushed over my cheek. "You have flour on you."

I sucked in a breath and pulled my face away from his touch. I couldn't have him touching me. Not when he was so close and I was so attracted to him.

"But you're right. I could have told you when we were texting. But I didn't want you to go to any trouble or worry about the state of the house." Then he moved past me into the kitchen. "I wanted you in your natural state. Mea culpa."

My natural state wasn't going to be of any particular interest to him, so I found his motives odd. But I was suddenly distracted by the sight of the suitcase he'd left by the front door. It was huge. That was no overnight bag.

Help me, Jesus, he was planning to stay for awhile.

"The house feels different," he said. "Lived in."

He went into my fridge and emerged with a soft drink, rolling his shoulders. Glancing around, I wasn't sure if he was upset with me or not. The kitchen did look lived in. The counter was scattered with baking supplies and the frosting was open and ready to be spread over the chocolate cupcakes.

"Are you learning the language of love?" he asked with a small smirk, gesturing to the laptop. His laptop. I had been using the computer that had been lying abandoned and collecting dust on the kitchen desk.

"It's just background noise." I started frosting the cupcakes. "I'll clean up as soon as I'm done with these."

"Don't worry about it. Do what you do. I'm not even here."

The look I shot him over my shoulder was incredulous. There was no pretending he wasn't there. Devin laughed out loud.

"It's very obvious when you're irritated," he said. "More challenging to tell when you're pleased."

I had been pleased ten minutes ago. Now I wasn't so sure.

"Why does it matter?" I had imagined him coming back to Richfield and me somehow impressing him. But I didn't know how to do that. He spent all his time with sophisticated women and I was just... not.

"I want you to be happy here."

Call me skeptical, but I didn't believe he really gave a shit. Why would he? He didn't know me. I was an employee. There had to be an angle, I just didn't know what it was. But I knew how to play the game. "Thank you. I am happy."

Frosting a cupcake, I watched him out of the corner of my eye. He had picked up the express envelope and was glancing through it. He didn't look surprised or upset by anything he was seeing. At one point he did pause on a particular picture and study it, a frown marring his handsome face.

"Something wrong?" I asked.

"Hmm? No, no, not at all."

So not believable, especially when he folded up the picture

he'd been staring at and slid it into his pocket.

Curious which picture he'd taken, I held out a cupcake in offering. "My first attempt at cupcakes. I can't vouch for how they taste."

Casually he tossed the whole envelope with all the other pictures into the trash receptacle next to the island and reached out for the cupcake. My eyes followed the motion. I looked at him in question but he just smiled.

"Thank you. I'd love one. I kind of have this sweet tooth, if you hadn't noticed."

I noticed a lot of things about him. Everything. "If it tastes awful you don't have to be polite. Just spit it out." Okay, that sounded way too pathetic. I decided to rein it in. Be normal.

Undoing the foil wrapper, he gestured with his head to the laptop. "So how is the French going? Seriously?"

"I just started. I thought I would listen to the entire book first, then redo it, stopping to do the written exercises for each chapter."

"That sounds very disciplined. But I have a feeling that's your personality." He put the cupcake between his teeth and held it there so he could free his hands to peel off his jacket. "Mm." He bit and chewed, holding the rest after he tossed his coat aside. "Good. Delicious."

Ridiculously pleased, that was me. The corner of my mouth lifted, I couldn't help it. He looked like he wanted to be alone with his cupcake. "Really?"

"So that's what you look like when you're pleased," he teased me.

My smile disappeared and I rolled my eyes, self-consciously.

"I'm glad you're using the kitchen. No one ever does."

Devin pinched off a piece of the cupcake and started to bend down to feed it to her.

"Don't!" I said, taking a step forward and grabbing his wrist. "Dogs are allergic to chocolate!"

He paused. "They are?"

"Yes. Deathly. It can kill them. I read it online."

"Oh. Jesus." He looked down at Amelia. "Sorry, sweetheart. I wasn't trying to murder you." He petted her head, bending down to give her a kiss. "I missed you, by the way. Yes, I did. But I guess I'm an idiot. Thank God we have Tiffany, huh?"

I was blushing and he knew it. God, seriously? Like my social life wasn't shitty enough? Now I had to act like a complete moron in front of my boss, Mr. Hot Shit? But first the weird envelope of pictures, then him showing up and scaring the crap out of me, had me thrown. I had been anticipating another night of being relaxed in a house I was starting to really feel comfortable in and now here he was, smiling at me and complimenting both my cupcakes and my common sense.

Besides, he looked so goddamn gorgeous, hair falling in his eyes, his beard scruff sexy and carefree. He looked like the men in movies who convinced a woman to fuck them in a restroom at a swanky restaurant. Hell, he probably didn't just look like that guy. He *was* that guy. I imagined him tearing Brooke's expensive dress off her lithe body and taking her against the nearest wall.

Ugh. I might not have any personal experience with that kind of lust, but I'd seen enough TV and movies to imagine it, and I was instantly sorry for the visual.

His presence definitely put me off balance. "I read it online,"

I repeated, because it seemed like I should say something. Then I went back to frosting cupcakes, which I had also read about online. I had attempted the swirl technique but I was pretty much sucking hard at it. Since I wasn't looking directly at him, I gathered the courage to ask, "So what's the story with those pictures?"

"Don't worry about it," he said. "Just some work stuff."

Oh, bullshit. That was no work packet. Unless his work was stalking himself. But I couldn't exactly press him on it. He was The Boss. A fact that seemed to keep hitting me over the head. He was from a totally different world, one of giving commands and demanding what he wanted. I was servant class. On the Titanic, I would have been on the lowest deck possible, and the first to drown.

But did he think I hadn't seen the picture of myself? I couldn't tell. He was hard to read.

"So what have you been doing since I was here last time?"

I shrugged, still frosting. "Reading, studying, cooking."

"Are you in college?"

"No. Not yet."

"Why not yet?"

"It's not practical." Meaning, I had no money.

"Have you talked to your grandmother?"

I paused, the unexpected reminder of my past making my stomach tighten. "No." I was surprised I hadn't, actually. I had thought she would get tired of doing things for herself, but apparently having to take care of the house solo was worth being rid of me. It did hurt, even though I didn't want it to.

I was finished with the cupcakes, and not wanting to stand

there and blink stupidly at him while he grilled me pointlessly, I started to fill the sink to wash dishes.

"You can just put those in the dishwasher," he said.

"I don't mind doing it." I didn't, because it allowed me to keep my back to him.

He didn't offer to help. But he did move over to the laptop and turn off the French lesson. That was an indicator to me he wasn't going to head to the master bedroom or to the family room any time soon.

"So you're reading *The Hobbit*?"

Glancing back, I saw he'd picked my book up and was studying the back. "Yes. I've read it before, but I'm rereading it."

"I read it in high school. A million years ago. I loved Tolkien, but I loved music more."

"So you always wanted to be a producer?" I asked, sloshing my hand around in the hot water to get the suds going. I was curious about his path to success. I hadn't found any evidence of him being music royalty, with family in the business before him. I'd briefly popped my head into his music studio at the back of the house upstairs but the equipment had been overwhelming and I'd been afraid to touch anything.

"That was something of an accident. I had visions of being a performer, but then it gradually became obvious that I am neither good-looking nor charming enough to be an onstage star. I'm much better behind the scenes."

What world did he live in that he thought he wasn't attractive?

I supposed a world of obscenely beautiful people. "Obviously it turned out all right for you."

"I was lucky in that I had some help. I met Owen Creed when

I was still an undergrad and he really opened some doors for me."

Devin had also married his daughter. I wanted to ask him about that relationship but I knew that was crossing a line. Personal curiosity aside, he was my employer, not my friend. Though I was well aware of the fact that I wished he were. "I'm sure there was luck involved, but you should give yourself credit too. He wouldn't have offered you his help if he didn't think you deserved it."

"More likely at first he did because I was dating his daughter and he was afraid we'd end up sponging off him for the next decade. He was determined to get me solvent."

I turned in the middle of scrubbing the mixing bowl to study him. He was wearing a smirk and I wasn't sure how serious he was. "I guess that's possible."

He laughed. "Well, there's that honesty I asked for."

"How does he feel now that you're divorced?" I went back to scrubbing.

"I think he feels guilty that he encouraged our relationship."

I wasn't sure what to say to that. Frowning, I turned the water on to rinse. What did that say about Kadence? Anything?

Without warning, Devin touched my arm. I jumped and turned. He had crossed the kitchen silently and was right behind me. "What?" I asked, panicked. He was crowding my space and I backed my butt up until it hit the cabinet.

"Stop with the dishes. It's annoying. Come sit down in the family room with me."

It was annoying? Was he serious? "Are they supposed to wash themselves then?"

"Put them in the dishwasher," he said shortly. He reached

over and yanked it open. Hard.

I stared at him, equal parts unnerved and pissed off. Diva.

But I'd spent enough years in obedience to purse my lips and keep my thoughts to myself. Nothing positive came from arguing. So I just started piling pots and a spatula into the dishwasher.

"Tiffany is displeased with me," he said, tossing his hair out of his eyes. He was wearing jeans and a dark green T-shirt, very casual.

It was some kind of game to him. Or maybe he was just mocking me. But either way, I despised being made uncomfortable. It wasn't fair, it wasn't honest, and just because I was the hired help, and the poor girl to boot, didn't mean I deserved to be treated that way.

"Tiffany doesn't like being yelled at for no reason," I told him, tossing his stupid use of third person back at him.

His eyebrows shot up. "You think that was yelling at you?"

I nodded, closing the door to the dishwasher and brushing my hair out of my eyes. Crossing my arms over my chest, I met his gaze, chin up, nostrils flaring. "No. But you said I'm annoying."

"I did not." He gestured to the sink. "All that banging around of pots, the water... it was distracting. You are not annoying. In fact, you are so not annoying that I want to talk to you, which is why the whole dishwashing thing was annoying. And you don't strike me as the overly sensitive type."

I didn't think I was, but sometimes you can only be made so aware of your place before it makes you angry. "Everyone has feelings."

"And I'm sorry if I offended yours," he said quietly. "Leave the dishes. Come sit down with me. I demand your company."

My eyebrows rose.

"I'm *requesting* your company," he amended.

"Why?" I asked boldly.

"Because I want to hear what you have to say. I'm surrounded by vain and silly people all the time and I'd like to have a decent conversation with someone."

"And you think I'm capable of that?" I wasn't sure I was. It wasn't like I had much experience talking to thirty-year-old men, but I did have an education and frequently made free with search engines. Part of me wanted to go a few rounds with him and see if I could hold my own. But mostly I was terrified I'd sound like an idiot.

"I think you're capable of just about anything you set your mind to." Devin shifted closer to me and for a second I could have sworn his eyes dropped to my mouth for a fleeting glance. I had to be imagining it.

But it wasn't my imagination that he brushed his arm against mine when he reached around me for another cupcake. His eyes challenged mine as his tongue plunged into the frosting. "You survived growing up on that rock, didn't you?"

Then he was gone, out of my personal space.

But the effect of it lingered in my body.

I had smelled him. Seen the stubble on his chin. Felt his hot breath. Watched his tongue dip suggestively into the creamy white frosting.

There was a burn starting deep inside me that he ignited, and I knew it was stupid, knew it was wrong.

So I met his gaze head on as he backed away, my voice steady. "Yes. I did survive. Sir."

Something about the words drew him closer to me again. His head went slowly back and forth. "But at what cost? You're not naturally a hard ass any more than I'm naturally an asshole. Yet look at us."

He put the cupcake up to my mouth. "Bite?"

"No, thanks," I whispered.

"Come on. Wine for me, milk for you. Is that what you'd like? Milk and cookies, little girl?"

If he wasn't naturally an asshole, he was doing a damn good job of being one.

Moving past him I bumped my shoulder against his before stomping over to the island to grab my cell and go down the hall.

To my room. Alone.

Where I lay on my bed on top of the covers and clutched my pillow to my chest, wondering why Devin had come back to Richfield. Why he had dragged himself away from Brooke's amazing abs to show up and ruin my contentment.

And to wonder if I would see Devin tomorrow and why my photo was being delivered via express mail to his isolated Maine compound.

The majority of my life I'd been wary, physically and emotionally protective of myself. The last month I'd had been able to relax my personal security system, had stopped doing figurative sweeps of the world around me with floodlights.

But now I felt not in danger exactly, just at risk. Of... something.

Falling for Devin. Losing control of my life when I had finally just achieved some.

My phone buzzed in my hand.

Figuring it was Cat, I was about to turn it completely off when I realized it was Devin.

My bark is worse than my bite. Good night, Tiffany.

All my anger disappeared. It wasn't a direct apology, but it was contrition. For a guy who walked around having everyone kiss his ass, it was a big deal.

So I texted him back.

Good night. Devin.

Using his first name felt good. Intimate.

My Google Alert went off.

Apparently Amazing Abs Brooke had gotten into a confrontation at the Prada store with Gold Daddy's ex-wife earlier that day. Entertainment news had the store video. You couldn't hear what they were saying but it was clear that Kadence was the instigator and when she lunged at Brooke, Devin intervened, stopping her from hitting his girlfriend. He then appeared to be calmly and rationally talking to Kadence, even putting his arm around her when she started crying.

The video cut out, apparently the story over now that the women were no longer scraping, and I was sorry I couldn't see the conclusion. Devin seemed compassionate, calm. Was that because he was still in love with his ex? Or was he a nicer guy than he liked to admit?

Or was I just trying to see what I wanted to see?

Either way, I was regretting my impulsive defection to my bedroom.

So I went back out into the kitchen, but it was quiet, dark. No sign of Devin or Amelia. I wondered if the Prada fight had been the catalyst for his early return to Richfield. The lights on the bottoms of the kitchen cabinets were on so the room was softly glowing. I saw the envelope sitting in the wastebasket and I fished it out, wanting to look at the pictures of Devin again. The beautiful women he spent time with. Remind myself that I was of no importance to him. He was being polite with me. He was bored. He was naturally curious. Nothing more.

But I flipped through the stack of photos twice before I realized one was missing. The picture of me.

He'd put one in his pocket. Had folded it up and slid it into his jeans pocket, right in front of me, and I had wondered at the time which one it was, and why. There were no other pictures missing but the one of me.

Devin had put me in his pocket.

I shivered, putting the envelope back in the trash and retreating to my room, shooting a glance towards the stairs, half expecting Devin to be standing there watching me.

He wasn't. The house was still.

chapter
five

"**M**ORNING," DEVIN SAID, WITHOUT LOOKING up from his laptop as I came into the kitchen.

He was still there. I was ridiculously pleased by that.

"Good morning." I yawned and shuffled over to the coffeepot, happy to see he'd brewed a pot already and half was still available. Happy also that he hadn't disappeared like last time. "Can I have some coffee?"

"No. You cannot have coffee." He shook his head without looking at me. "Of course you can have coffee."

Devin wasn't wearing a shirt with his lounge pants, but that was the only indication it was before eight am. He didn't look sleepy at all. He looked like he'd been tackling work for awhile, his eyes trained on the screen. "Don't annoy me by asking my permission for everything while I'm here."

Wow. He was starting the day off right where we'd left it. I got down a mug. "That's easy for you to say. You may not want to be annoyed or bothered or interrupted but I'm the paid employee, remember? I can't just walk around like this is my house."

"Your subservience makes me uncomfortable."

That pissed me off. "Then you shouldn't pay people to do things for you. End of story." I filled my mug and turned to him. "Because I can guarantee if I strolled around here back talking you and doing whatever the hell I pleased, you'd fire me. And since I need the money you pay, we're stuck with me being polite."

The corner of his mouth turned up. "Is that what you're being?"

Maybe not exactly, but hell if I would admit it. "Yes," I said flatly.

"Fair enough." He pointed his finger to the laptop in front of him. "Did you write this yourself?"

The blood drained from my face. "Write what?" But I knew exactly what he was talking about. Shit, shit, and shit. I had been using the house laptop to write some fictional short stories because it was way easier than on my iPad but I hadn't expected him to be home so soon. I had left it just sitting open in a tab on the computer when I'd stomped off to bed the night before.

"This story, 'Head Games,' about a girl who lives entirely in her own mind." His amber eyes studied me carefully. "I can't believe something so dark and intelligent and intriguing could come out of such a sweet-looking girl."

I didn't say anything, just hid my mouth behind the coffee mug. I had never intended for anyone to read the short story. Certainly not him, of all people. It was like splitting open my skull and allowing him to see my deepest, most inner thoughts. The ones that were murky and unpleasant and disobedient. The ones that ached and craved and yearned.

"Or did someone else write it?" he asked.

"No," I immediately protested. "I wrote it." While I didn't want him to read my secret work, my pride wouldn't allow me to let someone else take the credit for it. "I just like to make up random stories, that's all. When my grandmother was sleeping I couldn't leave the house, but it got boring. So I started writing. It's not a big deal."

Except it was. To me. But he could see right through my protests anyway.

"It's very well written. It's a complex story, unique."

His compliment made me feel warm, but at the same time, I felt like I couldn't accept it. "It's just okay. It wasn't what I wanted originally. It's… flat." Like my chest. Just no thrust to it.

"It's not flat. It's damn good, Tiff."

Normally I hated being called Tiff. It sounded childish. Like a temper tantrum. But from Devin it felt like affection. "Thanks." I was wearing skinny jeans, thick socks, and a sweatshirt. When I turned, embarrassed, intending to set my coffee down and get a bagel out of the pantry, I slipped on the hardwood floors.

My arms flailed for a second but Devin's hand shot out and gripped me hard, steadying me. He was just trying to be helpful, but the hot contact of his skin on mine sent a jolt through me and I yanked myself away, wincing.

It was instinctive, for multiple reasons. It was because I had been dragged, yanked, pulled, more times in childhood than I could count. A hard grip had always promised pain would follow and I had learned to flee, to hide. To anticipate and brace myself against anger.

It was also because his hand was big and firm and I was undeniably attracted to him. I didn't know how to deal with my feelings.

But the response was awkward, over the top, and he noticed. And called me out on it.

"What was that?" he asked.

"What do you mean?" I hedged.

"No. Don't do that." He slowly shook his head. "You said you'd be honest, remember? So tell me why you just jerked away from me when I was trying to keep you from falling on your ass."

"It was Pavlovian," I said, voice low, hoarse. I met his eye, defiant. I wasn't going to be ashamed of what other people had done to me. They were in the wrong, plain and simple. I hadn't deserved to be treated the way I had been and I wasn't going to be embarrassed.

"Why?" he demanded. "Because you were anticipating being hit?"

I nodded. "I had people get… rough with me as a kid. I was instinctively bracing myself when you grabbed me." Hearing the words out loud was enough to have me raising my chin even further in stubborn pride. "Don't feel sorry for me," I warned.

"Well, that's not very fair," he complained. "You demand I don't feel sorry for you, but if I callously disregard the fact that you jump like a kicked puppy, then what kind of heartless prick does that make me?" He crossed his arms over his bare chest. "Not great options you've left me, Tiff, so I think that I will have to defy you and tell you I feel empathy for what you've been through. I don't pity you, but I have compassion."

He was right. But I couldn't help it. Being looked at with pity was almost as bad as disgust, another response I'd gotten frequently as a kid. *What is she?* One foster mother had asked with blatant disdain. *Is she black? Mexican?* I had been thirteen and I had been overcome with hatred for her, for everyone who looked down on me, for stupid racism that had no basis in anything but ignorance. Hatred that I was made to feel inferior, less of a human being, because I was one of a handful of biracial people in the area.

I'd already had so many reasons to be isolated, separate from everyone. That she would throw the fact that I was biracial in my face like it was some kind of defect pissed me off.

So I had leaned in and whispered to her, "I'm your worst nightmare."

It was the smartest thing I'd ever done, because she freaked, and I had immediately been reassigned to Cat's family, one of the few places I had felt safe.

I felt safe here too at Richfield. Even with Devin there. Maybe more so with Devin there, whether or not that was logical. "Okay," I said simply.

"Can I touch your arm?" he asked, his voice low, compelling. "While you watch me do it. I'd just like to see that I don't scare you. I really don't like the idea that you could be afraid of me."

"Why does it matter?" I whispered, not sure I could just stand there and have him do whatever. Run his hand down my arm? I didn't know. I couldn't picture it. Aggression I knew how to respond to, gentleness I didn't.

"Because I like you."

My lip started to tremble. He didn't know. He couldn't know. To him, they were casual and simple words. An affection he'd expressed for a thousand people in his thirty years. For me, they were profound, powerful, agonizing. They weren't a slap or a criticism or a mocking tease. To my complete and total shame, they brought tears to my eyes. I fought hard against them but they blurred my vision and hung there stubbornly.

"Hey," he said softly, standing up and moving right in front of me. "Tiffany. Look at me."

"What?" I said, miserable.

"Come here."

Then he wrapped me into his arms and pulled me against his bare chest. Tense, I kept arms between us, but I did close my eyes and took a deep, shuddering breath, reining in my emotions. His body was warm and he smelled like cologne, a subtle, expensive cologne that made me want to lean against him. When his lips brushed softly over the top of my head, I shivered.

Devin put his hands over mine, and gently pulled them down so that there was no barrier between us. Our chests weren't touching, but I felt breathless, aroused, confused. Embarrassed by all my feelings. His fingers stroked mine, and one hand came up to wipe the tear that had escaped.

"Come for a walk with me and Amelia," he said, squeezing my fingers before releasing it and stepping back.

I was grateful that he wasn't pushing me for an explanation for why I had suddenly lost my shit and started crying. That he hadn't drawn out his compassionate moment. It would have just embarrassed me further. "I think you need a shirt first," I told him, sniffling a little and tucking my hair behind my ear.

He smiled. "Maybe the cold-hearted guy doesn't need a shirt."

I shook my head. "You're not cold-hearted. You're right, your bark is worse than your bite."

Devin winked at me. "Don't tell anyone. I'll never be able to control my artists if word gets out." Then he turned and whistled to Amelia. "Come help me find a shirt, puppy."

If that sentence had been directed at me, I was pretty sure I would have trotted after him willingly, tongue hanging out.

The thought of which made it even more embarrassing when he glanced back and said, "You, too. Come help me find a shirt."

"Excuse me?" He couldn't be serious. The thought of walking into his bedroom with him was horrifying. "No. Absolutely not."

His head tilted slightly. "I can't figure you out."

That was ironic. I couldn't figure him out at all. "There's nothing to figure out."

"Don't you trust me?" he asked. He sounded hurt by that fact.

Why the hell would I? I didn't know him. I didn't distrust him, not exactly, but I wasn't stupid enough to go to his bedroom with him. "No."

Suddenly he laughed. "Of course you don't. God, I'm sorry. You're probably thinking I'm going to lock you in my room and hold you captive for a decade."

I didn't see why any of that was at all humorous. I fought the urge to take a step backward.

But then he sobered up. "I'm sorry. I'm used to people doing whatever I want. Yet having nothing for myself. You're smarter than I am, Tiffany."

I shook my head. "I just assume bad intentions. Don't take it personally, please."

"I can go back to New York if I make you uncomfortable."

"It's your house," I said, shocked. "You have every right to be here. I can leave if you want me too. I can stay with a friend while you're here." How had we suddenly gotten there? I'd ruined the moment of closeness. Or imaginary closeness between us.

"That hardly seems fair to you. Especially since I hate this house."

Who could hate a house that beautiful? "You do? Then why are you here?" It was none of my business why he did what he did. He was eccentric. I'd already established that. But for some reason, his hesitation, his stance on the second step, shoulders stiff, made me feel like he was wrestling with something. That he was hurting, not physically, but emotionally.

"I don't know," he said simply. "Because fools rush in, I guess. And I've always been a first-class idiot."

"We all make mistakes."

"Somehow I doubt you do."

"There's still time." Because the truth was, I hadn't made any mistakes because there had been no opportunity to make any. I had no money, no freedom. Until now.

He gave me a smile. "I know you have no reason to trust me, but I won't hurt you, I promise. The house is monitored by surveillance cameras. Even if you don't trust me, you can trust that."

That was precisely what I was afraid of. Had he seen me doing searches on him online? How good were the cameras?

He clearly misinterpreted my silence. I was worried about what he'd already seen, not whether or not he was being truthful, but he came back down the two stairs he had climbed.

That made me uncomfortable. I wasn't sure what ground I was trodding on here, but it felt uneven. "I trust you."

I did. Everything I'd read about him online had reassured me that he was a decent guy. He had zero arrests, no public confrontations. He wasn't known to drink heavily, and while his ex-wife was often referred to as making a scene, he had spent a lot of time working with the Boys and Girls club, and donated a ton of money. I didn't think he was in Maine to molest me.

What I didn't trust was my ability to be normal around him.

I'd already almost cried and he'd felt the need to comfort me. What next? Would he see that I was attracted to him? Probably. Men like that knew. They could smell interest and use it to their advantage.

"Why am I here though, if there are cameras?" I asked. "Just to keep you in doughnuts?"

He smiled, standing very, very close to me, but not touching me. "You must think I'm such an arrogant ass. And in some ways you'd be right. But no, that's not why you're here. You're here because there is over a million dollars worth of shit in this house and the insurance company won't cover it against theft, fire, flooding, unless someone is in residence. So you're here to make sure the art and furniture I don't even like don't go up in flames or drown under a burst pipe."

That would have never even occurred to me. A shiver rolled over my skin. I glanced around, as if I could see dollar bills bursting out of the sofa cushions. I hadn't realized I was responsible for protecting so much.

"Oh."

"You didn't know?"

I shook my head.

"My assistant is usually more informative, so you take your duties seriously. On the other hand, Hattie likes to think she needs to keep all of my secrets." He raised his eyebrows up and down in mockery.

I remembered her comment about Devin not liking to come to the house, but no explanation as to why. "What secrets?"

"What are my secrets. Hmm. I hate the color yellow." He waved his hand in dismissal. "You don't want to dig around in my secrets and regrets. Boring."

"But why don't you like this house?" I asked again. If he hated it, why didn't he sell it?

For a minute he didn't answer and I thought he was either going to ignore the question or give me some sarcastic and flippant response. He was close enough to me that I could smell his light cologne, or maybe it was just his deodorant. See his bare skin, that golden chest, like the color of a roasted marshmallow, close enough I could reach out and touch it. I wondered what his body would feel like. All those muscles. All that hardness. My experience with guys was limited to a few skinny high school boys who had wanted to cram their fingers down my jeans while trying to inhale my mouth with vacuum lips.

They had been boys.

Devin was a man.

It intrigued me and terrified me at the same time. I wouldn't know what to do with him. It would overwhelm me. But that didn't stop me from craving him.

As I studied him, my chest rose up and down faster and

my lips parted without me realizing it. But he noticed. His gaze dropped down, swept over me, and my nipples hardened under his scrutiny. When he spoke, his tone was completely different. Not joking, teasing, mocking. But serious. Sincere.

"I never wanted this house. I wanted a smaller one. More like a cottage, a cozy place to escape to. But my ex-wife wanted this one because it's good for entertaining. What I didn't realize was that by entertaining she meant having sex with an aging rock star while I was in New York."

I winced, involuntarily. "I'm sorry."

"You are, aren't you?" he asked, puzzled.

His bewilderment puzzled me in return. "Why wouldn't I be? I'm sure it hurt you."

But he shook his head. "Most people take some small bit of satisfaction in knowing it happened to someone other than them. They feel smug."

Was that the world he lived in? I suppose it was the world I'd grown up in as well. How many foster siblings had I encountered who were grateful when I arrived and could take the heat off of them? But I still believed there were good people and I still believed in honesty and loyalty.

"I don't feel smug," I said truthfully. "I feel sad that someone would take the vow of marriage and then just screw anyone who showed interest in her. If someone loved me enough to want to marry me, I would be loyal to him. Day in, day out. I would live for him."

Devin reached out and touched my chin, cupping it with his hand, thumb stroking over my skin. I shivered. "And he would be a very lucky man, Tiffany."

For an agonizing second, as his amber eyes studied me, I thought he was going to kiss me. I felt the air shift, felt his body lean towards mine, felt my breathing slow and my eyelids drift lower.

But then he stepped back and the moment was over. "Wait here," he said roughly. "I'll get that shirt."

chapter six

EVIN THREW THE STICK FOR Amelia and we watched her bound after it. It was freezing outside, the wind sharp and biting. But it was what I was used to. "I wonder what it's like in Florida," I mused. "Is it like August here?"

"You've never been to Florida?" He was wearing a thick navy-blue coat, a knit hat on his head. I had no experience with wealth or luxury, but it was obvious everything he owned was expensive and well made. The stitching on the cuffs of his coat was straight, the hat free of fuzz.

I shook my head. "I've never been outside of Maine. Never outside of this area, actually."

"Really?" The thought seemed to horrify him. "No wonder you're so… untouched."

"It doesn't make me ignorant," I said defensively, cramming my hands in the pockets of my cheap thrift shop puffer coat. "I'm educated. And I can research anything on the Internet so it's not like I live in isolation." Except I did. Emotional and physical isolation.

"And do you always believe what you read on the Internet?"

"About the same way I believe what people say- after I've cross referenced it."

He laughed. "I actually meant it as a compliment. You're not... I don't know. *Harsh*."

"My grandmother would tell you otherwise. She told me just about every day what a mean ass bitch I am."

"Well, she must have deserved it then." Devin bent down and rubbed Amelia's head as she brought him back the stick. "Because I don't see anything bitchy about you at all. How do you see yourself?"

How could I describe myself to Devin? What was the truth? I knew myself, having spent the majority of my life in that isolation. No siblings, no parents, no family. Just me. I thought that despite the fact that I'd drawn a bit of a shit card I was playing the game pretty damn well. Being alone had taught me what was important, and that while I might not have money or a family, I had my intelligence, my belief system. No one else had to honor that code of values. But I did.

"I'm not bitchy," I agreed. "I'm honest. Fair. Loyal."

"I wish there were more people in the world like you then. You know, I never tell anyone about Kadence and Ricky," Devin mused as we walked down the driveway towards the coast, Amelia running ahead of us. "Something about your face makes me confessional."

Then maybe he could tell me why he was back at Richfield.

And if it had anything at all, even one tiny little bit, to do with me. "I won't tell anyone, obviously. You can trust me."

"I'm sure people know about her infidelity."

"*TMZ* doesn't."

He glanced over at me, surprised. "You've Googled me? Not that I'm surprised, I guess, but why?"

Heat bloomed in my cheeks and I watched where I was walking, rather than look at him. "I thought you'd be older when I took this job, so when I saw you that first night, I was curious how you got to be so successful so young."

Half-truth, but good enough.

He sounded amused. "Ironic, given that I thought you'd be older too. But Laura, my assistant, assures me you were an honors student in high school with no criminal record."

That tone was one that automatically put my back up. "Yes, I was an honors student. Don't make fun of me."

"What?" He held his hands out. "I'm not making fun of you. There is a difference between teasing and mocking, you know."

"I don't know you well enough," I told him flatly. The only people who could tease me were my friends, and those were Cat and Heath. Maybe my old English teacher, Mrs. Hutton, who had recommended me for this job.

"Then I guess we'll have to fix that."

Except there was a Lamborghini in the driveway that we were walking past. His car. I knew how much they cost. I'd looked it up. On the Internet.

Devin pulled his phone out of his pocket. "Excuse me, it's Laura calling."

The assistant.

"Hello?" he said into his phone. "It's cold. No. No. I'm not available. Then he can suck my dick."

Another minute and he was off the phone. "Sorry."

"For what?"

"Swearing in front of you."

Was he for real? Like I was five? Like he was the first one? "I can handle it. I'm not an infant."

But the look he gave me was dismissive. "Yes, you are. I can still smell the Similac on your breath."

I stopped walking. Just stopped moving, while he and Amelia kept going.

Finally he realized and paused, turning. "What? It was a joke."

"No, it wasn't. It was meant to put me in my place. I already know my place. You don't need to remind me of it." My whole life had been about people making sure I knew that I wasn't good enough, that I was inferior. Defective. "Don't patronize me," I said, my voice shaking just a little with anger.

I started to turn and go back to the house but Devin's voice arrested me. "Wait. Tiffany." His hand came out to grab my arm and halt my progress but he stopped himself, like he'd remembered my earlier reaction to being grabbed.

His contrition made me pause.

"How old are you?" he asked roughly. "According to my assistant you're eighteen."

"Yeah, I'm eighteen. But I've been taking care of my grandmother since fourteen, myself since five. I'm not your average eighteen year old."

"I know you're not. And I'm not patronizing you. I'm

protecting you."

That look…

My heart started to race and I forgot about the sting of the wind, the numbness in my toes. "Protect me from what?"

"From me."

A shiver rushed over me. "What do you mean? I thought you said I shouldn't be afraid of you."

But he shook his head and gave me a rueful smile. "Never mind. I'm just being moody and sulking. You don't have to be afraid of me. I did mean that."

Had he meant something more? That he was attracted to me? It was wrong to hope that, yet I was. I definitely wanted that, ridiculous and presumptuous and stupid though it was.

When he started walking, I fell in step beside him again. "Why are you sulking? Bad news?" It was still there. That tension between us. I didn't fully understand the dynamic, but I was starting to suspect it was sexual. Like he was attracted to me, but didn't want to be. Like my age was holding him back.

Or maybe it was nothing. Maybe I was imagining it because I wanted him to be attracted to me.

"I came here to escape the bullshit in New York, the whole scene. Fake people, users, cheats. Cristal and bottle service, award shows, crappy music that sells like gangbusters. I just need a breather."

I couldn't even imagine that life. "I would think the very things that drew you to the business could get tedious." I would despise those types of events. In theory, it would be fun to put on a cocktail dress and hit the town, and it would, one on one. But the whole small talk thing? I would suck at it. No experience.

"They do. I know no one who is broke would ever feel sorry for me and I don't expect them to. This is the life I wanted. I fought hard for my success because I do love the music industry. Taking raw talent and nurturing it... I love that. But I'm just tired." He gave me a smile. "I think I'm old."

"Maybe you just need to step back from the business end of things for a minute."

"That's why I'm here. To get the creative juices flowing again. I'm staying until right before New Year's Eve."

That was three weeks away. My pulse jumped and my nipples hardened. Just like that. Bam. The thought of seeing him every day for three weeks had me walking faster, excited. "I'm sure that will be relaxing for you and whatever." I wasn't sure why I added the whatever, but I regretted it. It sounded too young. Too high school.

"Don't say anything about you moving out while I'm here," he said. "There is no reason for you to do that. If you don't want to be around me, you can hide. You're not obligated to spend time with me."

"I want the company," I said. His company.

"Good. Me too."

We walked around his property in companionable silence, Amelia going for the stick Devin threw over and over again. It was hard to reconcile this man with G Daddy, the brusque and bored producer, traveling around the world on a whim and dropping thousands of dollars on dinner, jeans, his girlfriend.

His girlfriend. Brooke. I'd managed to forget about her.

I'd heard him be G Daddy with her on that awful phone call.

"I saw a picture of you online," I said. "I subscribe to a gossip magazine's online version and you were at the beach."

He glanced over at me in amusement. "You subscribe to a gossip magazine? That surprises me."

"I like to see what everyone is wearing. And I live in hope that someday I'll find a hairstyle that will make me look like Halle Berry."

"Why would you want to look like Halle Berry?"

I snorted. "Because she's beautiful."

"So are you."

"Whatever. I wasn't looking for a compliment." It embarrassed me that he might think I was.

"I know you weren't. That's not you. But listen, you are beautiful. Gorgeous actually. Never want to be someone else. Just be you."

Easy for him to say. "Being me wasn't exactly a stellar thing in a town that is all white."

"They were just jealous of your exotic beauty."

Oh, God. I was truly mortified. There was not a damn thing exotic about me. "Now you're really laying it on too thick."

Devin pulled me to a stop. We were almost back to the house. "No, I'm not. They're all ordinary and similar looking. Of course you stand out in a way that would make them jealous. And remember you told me I couldn't feel sorry for you. Well guess what? You can't feel sorry for you either."

Indignation rose in me. What did he know about how it felt to be me? Him of the perfect life and looks? "Where did you grow up?" I asked him.

"White Plains. Sue me." He reached into his pocket. "No, I didn't have a hard childhood. Yes, my parents funded my education. I have nothing to complain about. Even knowing that people use me, that I have no genuine friends, I recognize that I'm fortunate. Lucky, even. Is that what you want to hear?"

It made me feel guilty. He didn't know about my life. Conversely I didn't know about his. I wouldn't want people coming at me all the time the way they did to him. "I'm sure you have genuine friends," I said, feeling bad. "What about your girlfriend Brooke?"

That made him actually laugh out loud. "Brooke is not a friend. Or a girlfriend. She is someone I fuck."

The crude dismissal should have upset me, but the truth was, I was sickly glad to hear that Brooke meant nothing to him. "Oh."

"I don't suppose you've ever had someone in your life just to fuck, have you?" he asked, pointing the keys he'd pulled out of his pocket at his car to unlock it.

He was leaving. I shook my head. "No." I haven't had anyone to fuck, ever. I couldn't even imagine so casually sharing my body with someone. I knew a lot of people did and they had every right to do so. I just knew myself. I kept walls up to protect myself and if I was going to have sex with someone, it was going to be more than fucking. It was going to be intimate. I didn't want to do it just to do it.

"Stay that way," he told me. Then he opened the passenger door. "Get in."

I stared at him dumbly. "Where are we going?"

"Nowhere. Just a drive."

I hesitated and he made a sound of impatience. "What?"

"Is this an official duty?"

"What? No."

"Then ask me. Don't tell me." I wasn't his to order around. I wasn't anybody's. For the first time in my life I was well and truly free and I wasn't going to let anyone take that away.

I knew I was pushing it with him. But I had to start the way I was going to finish and keep what was mine- my pride.

Devin didn't fire me or throw me out of his house. He just shook his head. "Housesitter and manners coach. I'm being schooled by a child."

I opened my mouth to protest.

He held up his hand. "Fine. Not a child. And I'm sorry. Would you like to go for a drive with me?"

I nodded. "Sure. Thanks."

After Devin put Amelia in the house, he drove fast out of the garage, his body relaxed, hand comfortably on the gearshift. "When I was a kid I wanted to get out of White Plains so badly. It made me edgy, passionate, determined. It also made me drive too fast." He shot me a grin. "You like to drive fast or slow?"

"I don't have a driver's license."

"What?" He looked scandalized. "Why the hell not?"

His outrage made me smile. "Well. Because I wouldn't have a car to drive for one thing, after I got my license, or to actually learn how to drive in the first place. Plus you need your birth certificate to get your temporary license and I don't have mine. I could order it online but I never had the money and again, back to the whole lack of car thing."

"That's insane. How can you exist without a driver's license?"

"I seem to be existing okay." I was actually better than I'd been in a long time. "Don't sound so horrified."

"It is horrifying." Devin slowed the car down. We were still in his long driveway. "I'm teaching you to drive. Right now."

"What?" I stared at him, no longer amused. "No! I don't have my temps."

But he scoffed. "We're on my property. I'm not going to tell if you don't tell. We'll do a few practice sessions while you order your birth certificate."

"I... don't want to." How could I learn how to drive with Devin watching me? Knowing how outrageously expensive his car was?

"Oh, come on. Don't tell me you're afraid. I don't have you pegged as a chicken."

I was afraid. No question about it. But I didn't want him to know that. "Fine. But it's still pointless for me to have a license."

He put the car in park. "I can't believe you're walking around without an ID. How do you get anywhere? The airport, clubs."

I could see how that might be incomprehensible to him, but to me, it wasn't that big of a deal. "I don't. There aren't exactly a lot of clubs in Vinalhaven. And the only trip my grandmother would have allowed me to take was to hell."

"I'm sorry. I shouldn't be so shocked. You already told me you haven't traveled." He turned the car off. "Switch seats with me. Someday you'll be able to afford a car and you'll wish you had your license."

The whole thing seemed like a bad idea to me. "What if I wreck your car?"

"I have insurance." Then he reached over and tucked my hair behind my ear. "Come on. There's nothing you can even hit out here. It will be fine."

His casual touch had me willing to do just about anything.

"Fine. Whatever."

"I'm striking that word from your vocabulary. It goes to the graveyard of words right along with selfie." Though he sounded more amused than annoyed.

"Fine?" I teased.

He rolled his eyes. "Whatever."

I laughed. When I got out of the car and moved around the front of it, he passed me. Shifting so we wouldn't touch, I turned one hip toward the car. But Devin actually dropped his hand down onto my waist.

"Remember not to panic," he said. "You've got this."

Suddenly the driving seemed less dangerous than Devin himself. There was something about the way he looked at me, like I was important, that I mattered. Like he wanted to spend time with me.

"If I drive us off a cliff I promise not to say I told you so."

He laughed. "Thanks. That's big of you. But don't worry. I'm not going to let anything happen to you."

I shivered, but not from cold. He squeezed my waist. "Step one. Get back in the car."

He was actually a patient teacher. He pointed out all the important parts to the car and had me turn it on. Then put the car in drive and ease off the brake. We rolled forward.

"Oh my God, oh my God," I said, gripping the steering wheel so tightly my knuckles turned white. "This is the weirdest feeling."

"Now push the gas."

I did and we shot forward so fast both our heads snapped. I screamed and slammed on the brake, jerking us again.

"Whoa. It's okay. Don't stomp on the gas, just slowly press it down."

My heart was racing. "Okay. Okay, I've got it now." I took a deep breath and moved my foot, slowly accelerating this time. We crawled forward on the driveway. "Holy shit, I'm driving."

"You're driving. I told you it would be fine. You can probably stop making that sound now."

Huh. "What sound?"

"You're going 'oh, oh, oh.'"

My mouth snapped shut. God, he was right. I was. It was a weird little sound of distress.

"It's not really a sound I want a woman to be making when I'm with her."

"No?" I wasn't taking the bait. I was not discussing his sex life with him. It would only make me jealous.

"No."

I brought the car to a stop in front of the house and put it in park. I gave a sigh. One of relief and satisfaction.

"That's the sound I want a woman to make. Or at least one of many."

"Make up your mind," I told him, turning his sports car off and fingering the keys in my palm in exasperation. "Am I a kid or am I a woman? You can't have it both ways."

"You're an oxymoron, that's what you are."

Or just a moron.

I wasn't in danger of falling for him. I already had.

chapter seven

TWO DAYS LATER I WENT upstairs to ask Devin when he wanted dinner. I was having some weird sort of domestic high, cooking and cleaning for him. Sure, I was being paid for it. But I took total feminine satisfaction in watching him pack away whatever I cooked based off another Internet recipe. He ate all over the world in expensive restaurants and yet he had practically motorboated the biscuits and gravy I had made. It was never something I thought I would enjoy, but when you took care of someone who expressed gratitude for it, it was actually damn satisfying.

Cat had always encouraged me to pursue nursing, had said it came naturally to me. I had always figured it was just the only thing I had any experience doing. But now I was growing more confident in that choice because I liked the nurturing and orderly tasks of taking care of a household. Caring for patients would be even that much more satisfying.

It didn't have anything to do with the fact that it was Devin. Or so I told myself.

But I knew I was lying.

He was in his studio and I could hear his voice when I went down the hall, raised in anger.

Pausing near the doorway, I wondering if I should let him know I was there, or just come back later. But then his words gave me pause.

"I'm not doing this with you again," he said.

His tone was disgusted. "The fucking tears aren't going to work. You were totally out of line attacking Brooke like that."

So it was Kadence, his ex-wife, on the phone.

"It has nothing to do with her. I didn't get involved with her until after we split, you know that. I was never unfaithful to you."

Though anyone could say that, I believed him. It just seemed that while Devin was many things, cheater wasn't one of them, despite what those pictures said. It made sense to me that they were sent by his ex. Who else would have?

There was silence while he listened to her response, then I heard Devin give a sigh. "No. You're not throwing that in my face again. I don't believe you."

His voice was cold. Remote. "Prove it."

Trying to school my features so he'd think I had just gotten there, I put myself in the doorway, mouthing "sorry" that I was interrupting and backed up again to leave. He held up a finger to indicate I should wait.

"Of course I'll answer your call. I'll always answer your calls. But I'm not going to be manipulated." He was sitting at his desk and he had headphones around his neck. Yanking them off, he tossed them down. "I have to go. I'm not in New York and an issue has popped up."

Apparently I was his issue.

He said goodbye and hung up the phone. "Can I help you?"

Well, that was friendly. Not. "I just wanted to know if you wanted dinner soon."

"Don't look at me like that," he said.

"Like what?" I tried to neutralize my features, not really sure what my face was expressing. I considered myself pretty good at not showing my hand to anyone, yet Devin always seemed to read me really well. He knew when I was upset or nervous, or ticked off.

"Like I'm disappointing you."

"I don't know what you're talking about." I didn't. I wasn't surprised his conversation with his ex was contentious. How many people had awesome relationships with someone they had divorced? But he had seemed kinder to her on the video I'd seen, though I hadn't been able to hear what he was saying.

"I'm not a great guy, so don't give me credit for being one."

I just stood there for a second then I sat down on a love seat that had a zebra-striped fabric. Definitely not Devin's style. "What have you done that is so awful? You tell me I can't feel sorry for myself, well, guess what? Neither can you."

He gave a snort. "The minute I laid eyes on you I knew you were going to be a challenge."

It felt like a compliment, despite the words themselves. I pressed. "So what went wrong in your marriage? Besides the cheating, was it something else? You must have been in love at some point."

He fiddled with the keyboard in front of him, hitting a random key. "You want to hear about my marriage? Okay. Fine. When I met Kadence I was twenty-three and still totally naïve. I met her out one night in the Village and I thought she was so mature, so sexy. She knew everyone in the club and she spent money like a hundred bucks was a penny. People followed her around, including me. When she showed interest in me, I was triumphant. I won, right? At first I thought she was crazy fun, and crazy in bed. Then I realized she was just crazy. She'd lied to me about her age, telling me she was twenty six when she was really thirty two. I didn't care about the age difference, but it pissed me off that she'd lied. I found out by accident and I felt like an idiot. I broke up with her. But by then she was pregnant."

That wasn't what I was expecting. I cleared my throat. "Oh. Wow."

"So I married her. I married her even knowing I wasn't in love with her. Knowing that part of her made my skin crawl. How's that for romantic?"

It wasn't romantic, but it was admirable. "I think that actually disproves your theory that you're not nice. You married her because of your child and I admire that."

He made a face. "Don't. Don't ascribe admiration to me. I did it because I knew she was fucking crazy and I didn't want to condemn a child to living with her solo. I married her to be a shield. I didn't want her and I didn't really want a kid."

"Again, more reason to admire you for doing the right thing." I firmly believed that. "You could have walked away. Most men would have. My father did." It said a lot to me about his character that he'd done what he hadn't wanted to solely because he'd wanted to protect his child. "What happened to the pregnancy?" I didn't think he had a four year old. I'd seen no evidence of that online and he'd never once mentioned a child.

"She miscarried."

"I'm sorry."

But Devin shook his head slowly, leaning back in his chair. "I wasn't. Now tell me I'm a nice guy. Tell me you still admire me. I'm a fucking selfish bastard."

"A selfish bastard would have dumped her immediately upon losing the baby. Or had a string of affairs while tolerating his marriage." I leaned forward, wanting closer to him. "You're right, you know. Your bark is worse than your bite."

He gave me a small smile. "You're very good at throwing my own words back at me. I need to be more careful with what I say."

"I'm not meaning to throw anything at you." Myself included. The more time I spent with him, the more I wanted to though. My attraction was growing beyond just the physical. I felt drawn to Devin. I liked him. He reached inside me without even trying.

"I know." He studied me. "When I look at you, I don't see eighteen. I know that you're young, but you don't look young."

"That's the opposite of what everyone has ever told me. I think I look like a twelve-year-old boy." It was true. No ass, no boobs, short. I knew my expression must be incredulous because his words were ridiculous.

But he was insistent. "That's insane. Nothing about you is masculine. And you don't look young because you don't move like a kid, all random action and spastic energy."

The studio was windowless, with padded walls for

soundproofing, and it felt cozy, intimate. It was dark, the only light the one from his computer monitor. "Well, that's true. No one has ever called me spastic."

"Kids have this innocence about them, a sense of wonder and pure silliness, and for most teens that extends right through the first year or two of college. You don't have any of that."

I swallowed hard. "Life hasn't really been silly for me."

"No, I suppose not. You stare at the world like you've figured it out and found it all very lacking."

Maybe there was truth to that. I didn't really know. I did know that I wasn't angry. I also knew that I might display a tough outer shell, but inside I was soft and tender. "I'm not totally cynical."

"No, I didn't mean that. Just... wise. You're like my little owl."

I wasn't sure that was flattering or not. But I focused on his use of the word "my."

"Who?" I said, completely deadpan.

For a split second he didn't get it. Then he burst out laughing. "Good one."

I smiled back at him.

But then he got serious again, so quickly I wondered what thought had popped into his head. "What?"

"Part of me wishes you were immature, annoying."

"Why?"

"You know why. Don't pretend not to understand."

I knew what I wanted it to be. I said nothing.

"But you're not."

"I hope I'm not annoying."

His knee nudged mine. "Nope. Not even close. Are we friends, Tiffany?"

Trick question or not, I wanted to answer honestly. "I hope so. I want to be friends."

He rubbed his jaw. "I want a lot of things. But sometimes we can't have them."

"So we can't be friends?" It was like he enjoyed tormenting me. Dangling closeness in front of me, then taking it away.

"I think that it's impossible for us not to be." He looked away from me and at his computer screen. "Yes, I would like dinner."

It must be nice to be able to conveniently dismiss people. To be in control of jumping that fence from employer to friend and back again.

"I'm off duty for the day. You can come and help me though if you'd like."

He turned slowly back to me, clearly caught off guard. "You have balls bigger than some forty-year-old men, I'll give you that."

I pretended to glance between my thighs. "And yet I can still wear skinny jeans."

Devin gave a snort. "You're a stand-up comedienne tonight."

"I have my moments." I stood up to leave.

But Devin reached out and touched my arm. "I'll be down to help in five minutes."

I smiled warmly, glad he was conceding the point to me. "Good. I made cookies already."

He made a sound in the back of his throat. "God, you're killing me. For real."

The feeling was mutual.

"So where did you learn to shoot?" Devin asked me a few days later.

"Cat's dad, one of my foster fathers." I hefted the rifle on my shoulder as we walked out to his range. It was behind the garage and had the proper safety targets so no bullets would ricochet. "I was thirteen when I went there to live and I was four inches shorter than I am now, and about sixty pounds, I think. He figured I might need to protect myself some day." My boots crunched on the frozen ground. "He was a good man."

"Do you ever get to see him?"

"He's dead," I said shortly.

Devin put his hand on the small of my back as we walked. "I'm sorry," he said simply and I knew he meant it.

"Yeah. It sucks. Cat took it really hard."

"I don't know how you survived all those foster homes, honestly."

"I did, because I had to." I shrugged. "And I was one of the lucky ones. No one molested me or truly physically abused me."

"Don't downplay it."

"I'm not." We got to the target area. "I'm serious. I was lucky. It could have been a lot worse."

"That's how you learned to be so observant, isn't it?"

"Probably. Where did you learn to shoot?" I set down the spare bullets.

"It wasn't anything sexy, trust me. I did ROTC in college."

"How is that not sexy?" I gave him a dirty look. "I swear you do that on purpose."

"What?" Devin put headphones on me, clapping them in place over my ears.

I lifted one side so I could hear. "You pretend like you're not one of the cool kids. But you really are."

He tweaked my nose. "Don't talk back to your elders."

"I'm holding a loaded gun, Devin. Don't pull that age rank on me." It was what he always did when he got uncomfortable with our conversation. Our relationship. He pulled back and shielded himself behind my being eighteen.

I could appreciate that he needed a wall in front of him. I had one too. Mine was poured concrete. But it wasn't in place at his expense.

"You can be pretty bad ass when you want to." But he didn't back away. His gaze dropped to my mouth. "But you'd never shoot me. You like me too much."

He had me there. My breath created puffs of steam in front of my mouth as I watched him, wanting him to kiss me. Wondering if I had the nerve to kiss him.

Here alone, with no access or interference from other human beings, it seemed possible. But I had to remind myself that it wasn't reality. It was him and me hiding from the world, even though it hadn't been intentional. Here there was no G Daddy, and even though the signs of his wealth were all around us, it was easy to ignore the disparity in our lives.

We were friends. I wanted more.

"And you're avoiding the issue," I said.

"What issue is that?"

"My age."

"I'm not avoiding it. It's damn near all I think about." He took my hand and for a second I thought he was going to actually kiss me but he just briefly brushed his lips across my forehead. "Your hands are cold. Where are your gloves?"

"I only have mittens. Kind of hard to shoot with mittens." My voice sounded breathless.

He massaged my hand, and then together with his, slipped it into the pocket of his coat. It forced me closer to him, embrace open, my waist brushing against his. I wanted him so badly I didn't feel the cold. I felt hot everywhere, a burning intense desire that radiated from the inside out. In my right hand, I clutched the rifle, glad it wasn't loaded yet.

"What does it take to impress you?" he asked. "Just out of curiosity."

"Impress me?" It was a distracting question and I needed a second to drag my thoughts off what it would feel like to have his mouth on mine, his hands exploring the caverns of my body, stroking me to satisfaction. "What do you mean?"

"Who will be the man who earns your respect? Who earns *you*?"

Him. That's who. But I watched him watching me, his expression earnest. "A man who is loyal. Honest. Affectionate. I want to look at him and know instantly that he loves me. No walking on eggshells. I walked on those my entire life. I need to know where I stand."

I didn't really know where I stood with Devin. That was part of the problem. So whatever he was asking me, I was asking him in return.

"Anything else?" he asked. "Jewelry? Trips to Europe?"

I shook my head, my heart starting to race. Please let him be doing what I thought he was doing. "No," I whispered. "I don't care about any of that. I just want to be loved by a good man."

But something about what I said had him pulling back. He took my hand out of his pocket and gave it a final massage.

The gravel beneath his feet crunched as he took a step back. Disappointment rushed through me.

"You're right, you're not cynical," he said. "You're actually quite the secret romantic."

I supposed I was. It didn't seem like a lot to ask. I had never really felt unconditional love. Not in the way of a parent or a boyfriend. I had the love of a few friends, the affection of some classmates and teachers. Social workers who had expressed a great deal of concern for me. So if I was going to be involved with a guy, why should I settle? I wanted love.

Which was why I was suddenly grateful that Devin wasn't kissing me. I wasn't sure I could resist going there with him and yet, how would I feel afterward? I didn't want just sex. "Is that being romantic? Or just… aware of my own worth?" I asked him.

Something about my answer seemed to stump him. He opened his mouth, then shut it again. But finally he reached out, his thumb running over my lip. "And that is how you survived foster care," he said hoarsely. "Just so you know, I think your worth is priceless."

I reached for him, instinctively, watching to touch him, my hand rising to capture his. My heart was full and I saw admiration there, a genuine, deep affection for me.

But he dropped his hand before I could clasp him. "So priceless in fact, I don't think I can afford you."

"What is that supposed to mean?" I whispered, disappointed.

"Hold out for that good guy, Tiff." He squatted down and fished a handful of bullets out of the box. He loaded his rifle with sharp, angry movements. "That's all it means. Nothing more. Nothing less."

He didn't think he was good enough for me.

The very thought stunned me. Made me incapable of speech.

It was laughable, insane, ludicrous. I wanted to step forward, to tell him that he needed to know his own worth, too. That he wasn't a bad guy, or selfish, or greedy. That he was generous and thoughtful. Surly, yes. Bad, no.

But before I could gather my thoughts, he said, "Stand back."

I did.

He aimed and fired.

The shot shattered the quiet of the afternoon.

I winced instinctively.

And that was the end of our conversation.

When he paused, it was clear he'd hit the target dead center.

When it was my turn, my aim was high.

chapter
eight

*C*OME UPSTAIRS. I WANT YOU *to hear something.*

I paused in the middle of chopping vegetables for a salad as I read the text from Devin. He was in his studio again, like he had been every day for the last few weeks since he'd arrived at Richfield. The days had settled into a pattern. I would wake up and he'd already be in the kitchen, drinking coffee and working, sometimes on his computer, sometimes on conference calls. He would wave me over and he would set everything aside while we sipped coffee and talked for twenty minutes or so. Then he would go upstairs to his studio, emerging only for lunch. By dinnertime, he was done and we would go for a driving lesson, then I would cook for him, with him acting as sous chef. At night we talked, played chess, made a fire.

I waited for him to get bored with me and go back to New York or at least start going out in town, eschewing my company for random strangers in restaurants or bars. But he didn't.

He sought me out, repeatedly. I hung back and waited and every day, he inserted his presence into my day. He dominated and demanded my attention and I craved it. He made me feel like I mattered to his day. That I brought him some sort of pleasure with my conversation, my cooking, my existence. His moods became darker as the days went by, and I knew that he had made his mind up that he couldn't be more than a friend to me. That he had decided I needed to wait for a guy my own age, with some ten page laundry list of virtues that I was pretty sure didn't exist in one man outside of Jesus.

But I was willing to wait. To bide my time until Devin either returned to the city or he realized that more than friendship was brewing between us. We finished each other's sentences. We sparred and discussed and challenged each other. We were deeply and undeniably attracted to each other, our casual touches too lengthy, too charged, to be fully innocent.

We were living together, yet we weren't together. We had a nebulous unexplainable relationship that wasn't a relationship, exactly. We weren't boss-employee. We crossed too many lines for that. We weren't romantically involved, technically. Yet we said things you didn't and shouldn't say to someone when your relationship was purely platonic. We were friends, as much as you can be when someone is paying you and they waffle between treating you like a little buddy and someone they wanted to devour with their mouth. I knew Devin saw me as an equal but then he would call me his "ma petite amie" or explain something utterly stupid to me, like where Budapest was in Europe, and I would be forced to admit that he wasn't going to stop, no matter how times I called him out on it. He needed to use my age as a shield between us, otherwise he'd have me up against a wall kissing me witless.

I was torn between gratitude that despite his questionable methods he was keeping that barrier intact between us and frustration that he didn't just fucking go for it. Would I really regret it if we blurred that line between friendship and love?

Whatever you wanted to call it, whatever we were doing, it made me wake up every day eager to see him. Our conversations were exciting, stimulating. I laughed more than I could ever remember laughing.

And if I was falling in love with him, that was my problem. My mistake. I would get over it when he left. But for now, I wanted to enjoy it. We were edging closer and closer to the point when we wouldn't be able to stop, and with each day that went by my fear of the consequences grew smaller and my desire grew larger.

I went upstairs and found him in his studio, headphones on, computer in front of him. He had mixers and soundboards and other things that lit up and looked intimidating as hell all turned on. He looked up when I went in and smiled at me. It did me in every time. It made me as ridiculous and inane as every girl I'd ever made fun of for going gushy over a guy.

"Hey, how is the writing going?" he asked.

I was attempting a full-length novel and was about thirty pages into it. It was a horror story about zombies. How they craved and took and sought and begged for everything you had, and were never satisfied. Like so many people I'd met in my life. "I just wrote a couple of pages. I'm not feeling it today. I keep thinking about Christmas." Five days out. I'd never decorated for Christmas but I was itching to go back to Cat and Heath's and crash there for a few days and do the holiday up right for a change. With food, and a present or two. I'd never done that.

"Christmas?" Devin looked at me blankly. "What about it?"

"I was thinking I would go to Cat's house. But I should stop in town first and buy some presents and food. Can you drop me off at the ferry?"

Now he was frowning. "Are you saying you're leaving for Christmas?"

Perching on the edge of his desk, I frowned at him. "Well, yes. I mean, you're going to New York, right? It's okay if the house is empty for twenty-four hours, isn't it?" I had pictured him either going to his parents' house or doing some sort of friends' celebration at his apartment. He'd been gone for weeks and the phone calls had gotten more frequent, his tone with his team more impatient as they clearly pressed for his return.

"I'm not going to New York."

"Oh." That surprised me.

"And if you're there..." he flicked his hand in the general direction of the ocean. "Then I'm here alone. So no, you do not have my permission to go to Cat's house."

I felt my jaw drop. "For real?" I couldn't believe he was going to pull that employer crap with me. Why did he care if I went to Cat's?

"For real," he said, sounding petulant. "I want you with me."

My cheeks grew warm and I went very still, butt resting against his desk, legs near his arm. He wanted my company. He could do anything and anyone frankly and yet he wanted to stay there at Richfield with me. It meant more than it should. "You do?"

Because I wanted to hear him say it again. Because I needed to hear him say it again.

"Yes, I do. I *desire* you… to be with me." Devin reached out and took my hand, stroking my fingers with his. "I got you a present, you know."

Did that mean he was capitulating? Was he giving in to the chemistry between us, finally? I would stay if that were the case. "Oh. I guess I should stay then," I said. I couldn't say no to him. Or to a present. Or to any indication that he had abandoned the ridiculous notion that I was too young for him. That he might realize I was important to him, as more than a friend. "I didn't get you a present." I gave a nervous laugh. "I don't really know how to give presents."

I didn't. I hadn't since I was a kid and I'd made a potholder at school for my grandmother and she had scoffed at it. That rejection had stung more than any of the smacks, the swats, the screaming. It had been cruel and I wasn't sure that I knew how to be vulnerable enough to give a present anymore.

But then again, I was nothing if not vulnerable with Devin. I basically had ripped my beating heart out of my chest and handed it to him. While allowing him to pretend that we were just friends, him my boss.

"You don't need to get me a present. I have everything I want. You could bake me something though and I wouldn't complain."

That made me relax. "I could do that." Him and his sweet tooth. It was a good thing he could afford stellar dental care.

But I'd turn his kitchen into a goddamn bakery if it got him to cross the line he'd drawn so carefully between us.

He went from stroking my fingers to lacing them through mine so we were actually holding hands. "You don't mind staying here, do you?" he asked. He had sat back in the chair, and his legs were open. I wanted to wedge myself between his knees and climb onto his lap.

"I don't mind." I also didn't mind how freely he touched me.

"Good. Listen to this song I'm working on. I created it with you in mind."

"What do you mean?"

"I wanted to capture you. If you were a sound this is how I hear you. Light and innocent and dark and gripping all at the same time."

He'd written a song for me? That was seriously hot. Seriously sweet. Seriously romantic. Or maybe it was akin to being inspired by your family dog or by a bus accident or crawling spiders. It could mean anything.

But that was a lie I told myself for protection. I knew what it meant. I knew that he had feelings for me. When you spend your whole life never having anyone give you that look, you damn well recognize it when it's shown to you. He cared for me. He knew it. He just wasn't willing to say it in those words.

"I'm not sure if that's a compliment or what," I said. "I'm both light and dark?"

"Not dark in an evil way, but mysterious. With depth." He brought our hands still clasped up and tapped his knuckle on my head. "No one really knows what's going on in there, do they? It's a secret garden. That's the title of the song-'Her Secret Garden.'"

I heard both the compliment and the sexual innuendo loud and clear. God, I wanted this to finally be it... when he wrestled his doubts into submission. My doubts had evaporated.

There was nothing but me between the desk and Devin, me open and unable to hide my emotions. The things he said weren't stupid pick-up lines. He wasn't obvious and crass or anything that I could dislike or dismiss. His flattery was like ivy, it crept around the edges of my defenses, wrapped them, and overcame them. He smothered me with a commanding kindness. It wasn't always nice, it was sometimes selfish, but it was honest.

My wall had been forced down, gradually and ironically, while he was struggling to build his higher. Maybe that was why. Because I knew he wasn't trying to get in my pants, or use me and toss me aside, or have me fall for him as a pure ego stroke the way a guy in high school had. While he fought his feelings, I was able to slowly and quietly embrace mine.

"I guess that's better than 'Damp Basement,'" I said. I meant it as a joke. Though as usual my delivery was dry.

But Devin shook his head. "Don't. Don't undermine yourself. Please. Even if you're kidding."

I swallowed hard.

He stood without warning, filling the space immediately in front of me, a hard masculine wall rising before me. I looked up at him in question, wondering if I should pull my hand away from his. Not wanting to.

"I keep trying to find flaws in you," he said. "I've been working really hard at it because it's really, really inappropriate for me to find you attractive. But I do. Does that make me a fucking pervert or what? You're too young."

He sounded anguished.

"Devin. Stop. You said yourself there is nothing young about me." I shook my head, overwhelmed by how much I wanted him to kiss me. "I'm an old soul. I'm no carefree teenager. I may not have world experience, but I'm not innocent. And I find you attractive too."

I wasn't sure where the courage to say it out loud came from, but I figured it wasn't exactly a mystery. Anyone would be able to see that I was hot for him. It was more than that. I was falling in love with him. I wasn't uncomfortable with our age difference. A guy my own age was never going to appeal to me with his stupid bragging and potty humor and fascination with random breasts. Those guys would never impress me or hold my attention. So the age difference definitely wasn't what bothered me about Devin.

If there was anything that gave me pause, made me uncomfortable, it was his wealth that did, his lifestyle. He came from a different world entirely from me, and here, hidden away at Richfield, he might want me on some level. In the real world? He wouldn't. I knew that.

Or he might want, but he wouldn't act on it. Not with prying eyes and nosy media and online bloggers and trolls ready to eviscerate anyone who did anything they could take a jab at. If Devin busted me out in public, he would be thrust into the limelight in a way he would despise. Or maybe he wouldn't. Maybe no one would give two shits what a rich guy did with a girl who was legally of age. I guess it depended on whether or not Devin wanted to take that risk. Any risk. For me.

So I just stood there and waited, studying his beard scruff, wanting to touch it. To touch him. Everywhere.

His free hand snaked around behind my waist and he did something at the computer. The music filled the room. It was electronic, ultimately a dance song for a club, yet it was more than that. It had nuances and layers. It was raw and emotional, pounding, anguished. Was that how he saw me? Or as he put it, heard me?

Cupping my cheek, he caressed my skin and I sighed. I had been getting bits and pieces of that touch, that tender connection, since the minute he'd arrived at Richfield. I craved his touch now. I wanted more. I wanted all of him.

"I keep thinking that I have no right to keep you here, like this. But I can't stop myself. I can't let you go. It's selfish, but I'm tired of being reasonable. I spent four years being reasonable. Now I just feel defiant."

"What are you trying to tell me, Devin?" I asked, because I had to hear it. I had to know. We could dodge and weave around the sexual tension between us forever. Though there was more to it than that. It wasn't just about desire. Sex. We couldn't pretend that our feelings were just simple and platonic friendship.

"Just this."

And he bent down and kissed me.

I kept my eyes open until the very last second, because I wanted to watch the desire in his gaze, I wanted to let him see mine back, before allowing them to drift shut. He was a beautiful man, features strong, unusual. Maybe he wasn't traditionally attractive, but to me, he epitomized a strong, sexy man. His mouth brushed mine, briefly, not tentative, but teasing. Just a hint, a whisper, then he was gone, lips hovering over mine, his warm breath caressing me. His thumb stroked my cheek and he kissed first the right corner of my mouth, then the left.

"God," he breathed. "I've been wanting to touch you so much.

I've been fantasizing about kissing you. But I didn't want to ruin things. I didn't want to take what I don't deserve."

Giving in to my urge, I pulled my hand from his and slid it up his chest, feeling the contours of his body. He was warm beneath his T-shirt. Hard. Sighing in pleasure, I kept going, up to his beard scruff. It was softer than I expected. He was watching me, not speaking, his grip on my waist tightening. Instinctively, without thought or planning or concern for the consequences, I moved my hand into his hair, and guided his head back towards mine.

That hadn't been enough. Not after three weeks of teasing.

This time, I kissed him, and it wasn't light. It was a desperate, urgent press, lips open. He groaned in the back of his throat right as the music swelled around us in a fast-paced crescendo. Devin yanked me against him and I collided with his chest, felt his erection against my thigh. Desire clouded my judgment, yet fear prevented me from fully falling over the edge of no return. More than a kiss was more than I could handle until I knew what we were doing.

I tore myself away from him, panting, fingers gripping his shirt. "I like this song."

He gave a harsh laugh. "God, you're killing me. Now go away before I do something we both regret."

He sounded surly and bitter. It made me smile. "What would I regret, Devin? Explain it to me."

"This. Us."

"What us? Us kissing? Or more than that?"

He gave an exasperated groan. "Tiffany. Leave me alone."

That was so ridiculous I knew there was no pressing him any

further right then. He had retreated behind his emotional wall.

So I let it go. It was enough that he'd kissed me, enough that I could still taste him on my lips. Enough to know that slowly, surely, he was caving.

"Sure. I'm fixing lunch if you want to come down and eat."

"No, I do not. I'm busy." He physically shifted me away from him.

I ducked my head so he wouldn't see my possibly smug smile. He didn't trust himself around me, and that was seriously hot. Plus he was working on a song inspired by me. "Can I at least meet Cat in town then? I can ride my bike."

"It's twenty degrees outside."

"I'll be fine."

"I'll drive you." He had sat back down and crossed his arms, a scowl on his face. "Give me two hours."

"Thanks." Then with a boldness I didn't know I had I bent down and kissed him again. It was meant to be a light tease, a thank you, a see you in a bit, but Devin put his hand firmly on my ass and hauled me up against him.

He devoured my mouth. He kissed me like he hadn't touched a woman in a decade. Like I was everything.

I clung to his shoulders and let him sweep me under, with his lips, his tongue. He teased, he took, he tasted, and no fumbling kiss I'd had before could have ever prepared me for that. I felt it everywhere. From the roots of my hair to my tingling breasts, to my aching inner thighs. I felt alive, my skin sensitive, body deeply and fully aware of him.

He broke off and studied my face, his breathing heavy. "You have two choices. Go downstairs and make lunch."

When he didn't continue, I raised my eyebrows. "That's only one choice."

But he shook his head, his eyes dark and full of lust. "The other one isn't an option. Never mind."

"Why not?" I knew what he was thinking, knew him so well now I could practically hear his thoughts. Option two was I could climb on his lap and we would have sex, right there, right then.

He was right. It wasn't really an option. I wasn't ready for that. I wanted to with every fiber of my being. But at the same time I was terrified. My experience was too limited for this position. For now.

"Sometimes I have the ability to stop my selfish tendencies. Not always. But sometimes. One step at a time, ma petite amie."

He'd retreated to the friend title again. I could live with that. Because he was right. One step at a time.

But what he wasn't realizing was that I had infinite patience. I'd spent day in and day out for the last four years taking care of an old woman who hated me and I hadn't gone insane. I could wait for him to grapple with his conscience and conclude that he could have sex with me and still live with himself.

Given the look on his face, I wouldn't have long to wait.

"I'll bring you up a sandwich," I said, shifting out of his touch.

His sour look almost made me laugh.

He turned back to his computer. "You're dismissed, Tiffany."

Asshole worked well on him. There was no way I was going to let it affect me though, not when I knew the truth. "Of course, Mr. Gold. Let me know if there's anything you need."

The look he shot me was filled with desire. "We're not doing this. We can't do this."

"What is that?" I asked, faking innocence. "What are we doing?"

He made a sound of exasperation. "You know what I'm talking about."

Of course I did. We'd been heading towards this for weeks. But he had to say it. He'd yet to say it. And I wasn't filling in the blanks for him.

He leaned in, then tore himself away. He was fighting against it because he was afraid of other people's opinions, or maybe his own morality. It was possible he was worried he would hurt me. That I would assume too much. Become a clinger. Maybe he didn't know what he wanted aside from what he thought he couldn't have.

"Using last names again?" I asked, staring at him boldly.

There was more than one way for me to put us on equal footing. He wasn't going to put this on me. It was his choice. Mine was already made.

"No, we're not using last names." He rubbed his jaw. "Beyond that I don't have a fucking clue."

"Yes, you do." With that, I left the room. He was in. I could feel in the shift of his body towards me. That wasn't a one-time kiss. He wanted more. He wanted me, beyond just the physical. Maybe in spite of me physically not being his type.

Let him define us later.

For now, I would just wait and let him be the boss.

In every sense.

"*H*E'S PLAYING WITH YOU," CAT told me bluntly, sitting across from me in the coffee shop.

"Cat, that's a little harsh," Heath told her, looking shocked. "I'm sure Tiffany knows what she's doing."

I was telling them my plans to stay at Richfield for Christmas and it had not gotten a positive reception. I hadn't given full disclosure but I did admit there was something going on between us, I just didn't know what. Cat's assessment of Devin made me blush with anger and humiliation. "I'm not an idiot. I know that he's not going to marry me," I said. "He's bored, he's feeling restless and over the whole New York thing. We're alone together all the time and I'm a novelty. A nut he wants to crack." I ran my finger over the rim of my coffee mug. "The weird shut-in girl. He just finds it fascinating that I haven't been more than twenty miles away from home my entire life."

But he did genuinely like me. I believed that without a doubt. Yet something about her reaction made me want to keep the true nature of my feelings a secret. It was just between me and Devin. It was too new, too fragile, too... special. What happened at Richfield was our world, our secret, our relationship.

"I'm sorry, I don't mean to be a prick about it," she said, sounding contrite. "I'm just worried about you."

"I know." I did. And she was right to be worried. I knew it. Even if it made my chest tight and my palms sweaty. I knew that eventually Devin would go back to New York and I couldn't go with him. "But while I might fantasize, I'm not an idiot. I'm going to take advantage of an opportunity that might never present itself to me ever again."

"You're always saying she's practical," Heath said to Cat.

Then he studied me. "But Tiffany, seriously, you don't have the experience this guy does. You might get hurt, you know."

"Oh, I think it's pretty much a guarantee I'll get hurt." I smiled at them. "But I know what I'm doing. For whatever reason he does like me, for now. Today. Tomorrow or the day after or the day after that he'll get tired of me. I know that. But I can't help it. He fascinates me."

He did. I knew his scent now, his laugh, his movements, expressions. He was surly and brusque, but he was also kind and generous. He was an introvert in an extroverted profession, and mistakenly or not I felt like he showed me a side not everyone saw. The real Devin. Not G Daddy. And I liked Devin. I liked him in a way that my insides warmed when I saw him, and my thoughts went all soft and sweet, like I was continually stroking a kitten. I wasn't a sentimental person. Heath was right about Cat's assessment of me. I was practical.

But Devin brought out something more in me. He made me feel like a woman. Like all of those feelings and needs and desires that I had suppressed couldn't be contained anymore. They had to breathe, out in the open.

Cat sighed. "Everything in me is saying run away as fast as you can. But I know you. You've made up your mind to stick it out."

She did know me. "I have."

"Even knowing you'll get hurt?"

I had a card to play and I pulled it. "Did the possibility of getting hurt stop you from being with Heath?"

"Whoa," he said. "How did I get pulled into this?" Heath was a fisherman and a former Marine, and he was wearing a flannel shirt. Not the hipster variety with skinny jeans, but a working man's flannel. He put his hands up before reaching for his coffee. "I say do whatever you want except for any illegal drugs."

"That's your advice?" Cat looked at him in exasperation. Then to me, she gave a half smile. "And no, nothing would have stopped me from being with Heath. But that was different."

"How?" I wasn't trying to be a bitch any more than she was trying to be a prick, but that was bullshit. We all entered into a relationship, or whatever the hell you wanted to call it, with someone knowing there was a very distinct possibility we could get hurt. I knew Devin was going to return to New York and forget I existed. For the most part. But Cat had gone back to Heath after he had disappeared on her for four years, so what was the difference?

None.

"He's rich. And older."

"I am?" Heath joked.

Cat made a face. "Guys like that do whatever they want."

"I think he just walked in," Heath commented in a low voice.

"What?" I swiveled around. He was right. Devin had walked into the shop, and was impatiently sweeping his gaze around the room. I raised my hand in greeting when he spotted me. "I wonder why he's back so soon."

I had only been there for forty-five minutes and he'd said he would be back in two hours. The coffee shop was a local place, not a chain, and it was filled with moms, fishermen, and retired people. Devin stood out from the regulars and a half dozen pair of eyes watched him cross the room. The one thing he didn't have to worry about was someone local reporting his movements to online media sites. Mainers were big on live and let live. They wouldn't give a shit what a guy from New York was doing, though they would stare at him suspiciously.

"What does he want from you, seriously?" Cat asked, urgently. "He could have sex with anyone."

"Exactly," I told her. "He could. That's not what he wants. He wants a friend."

"With benefits."

Yes. But it was more complicated than that. I thought. I shot her a look that was meant to mean "behave" and glanced back to smile at him.

When he reached us, he put his hand on the back of my chair. "Hey, Tiff." Then he turned and introduced himself to Cat and Heath, sticking his hand out to shake.

Heath stood up to meet the handshake firmly and I felt them sizing each other up in that way that guys do. I looked to Cat in amusement, but she was making a sour face at Devin. I could tell she was shocked by his appearance. She knew he was thirty, but I had reassured her he wasn't anywhere near approaching creeper status. There were different kinds of thirty, though, and Devin didn't have a boyish face. It was the kind of face that would have looked mature for his age even at fifteen. He didn't have dimples or sparkling eyes or a boyish charm. He was all rough edges and hard angles. He was the boss. It was obvious.

After everyone had said hello, he glanced at the table in front of me. "You're not drinking any coffee?"

I shook my head. I'd only brought five bucks and I'd already drank it in the form of a latte.

But Devin knew me well enough to see through that. "You're

a coffee junkie. What do you want? I'll go get it."

"I'm fine."

He rolled his eyes. Then asked Cat and Heath, "Do you need anything?"

They shook their head. "No, thanks," Cat said.

He squeezed my shoulder and went to the register to order. I was blushing. I could feel the heat in my cheeks. I wasn't even sure why. Maybe it was just that Devin had been my secret until an hour ago. Having my friends meet him made my infatuation feel as foolish as they seemed to think it was.

I didn't look like I belonged with him. I looked like the kid he was fostering in the Big Brother program, despite what Devin said. He saw me differently from everyone else.

"What are we supposed to say to him?" Cat whispered.

I shrugged. "Anything you want."

"Can I ask him if he knows Beyoncé?"

"Very funny."

"What?" She smirked at me. "He knows celebrities. Don't tell me you haven't asked that."

"I haven't. He has occasionally mentioned people in passing, but he uses their real names, like Sean and Stephanie and Lizzie, so I think I know who he's talking about, but I'm not going to ask. It's awkward."

"It's crazy, that's what it is." Cat shook her head. "I don't know about this."

"Having money isn't a crime." A glance over at the register showed Devin checking his phone while he waited for our drinks. It didn't escape my attention that he hadn't asked me what I wanted. I was curious if he'd get it right though.

"The way you're looking at him…"

I looked back at Cat. She was frowning, her brow furrowed. "What do you mean?"

"You're in love with him. Oh, my God."

I was. I knew I was. I had been falling in love with him gradually since the second I'd met him. But it wasn't relevant. Not yet. "So? That doesn't change anything."

"Be careful," she whispered urgently.

Shrugging, I told her, "I know what I'm doing."

Devin pulled out the chair next to me and settled his long legs under the table. He handed me a cup with a smile. "Your caramel latte."

"Thank you." He'd gotten it right. He had noticed what I tended to make for myself with the Keurig at home. At Richfield. At his house. God. I was thinking of his house as my home.

Cat was right. I needed to be careful.

But he was so beautiful. So commanding. So intelligent.

I wondered if my face showed everything I was feeling.

Maybe I wanted it to. Maybe I wanted to nudge him past what he'd started in his studio.

It must have shown something because Devin's smile evaporated. He reached out and tucked my hair behind my ear. Still looking at me, he said, "You don't mind if I steal Tiffany for Christmas, do you?"

With major effort, I tore my gaze from his to look at my friends.

Cat looked horrified. Heath looked puzzled.

I knew exactly how they were feeling. They were my feelings too.

Devin chatted casually with my friends, asking Heath about his fishing boat, and Cat about her plans after college graduation. He didn't name drop or talk about the city. He shared how he'd spent summers in Maine with his grandparents, and that's why he'd decided to buy a house there as an adult. He wanted the same idyllic summer nights.

While he spoke, his hand drifted over to my knee, resting there on my jeans. He shifted his chair closer, spread his leg so it was touching mine, his body warm and hard through our respective denim pants. His fingers stroked my kneecap, then gradually began an ascent up my leg, my thigh, caressing the whole way, casually, intimately. It was normal for him to touch me, but not in public, and never quite as absently as he was. Like he was doing it without thinking. I didn't get the feeling it was sexual in that he wanted to turn me on or get me off, though the first he was, and the second he might. It was more that he felt comfortable with me to the point it was natural.

A guy my age would have taken it too far. He would have stroked right up to the seam of my jeans below the zipper, or shifted my own hand onto his erection under the table. Devin didn't do that. When he was perilously close to inappropriate, he retreated, giving my knee a final squeeze before removing his hand.

"Too bad I'm never here in the summer," he said with a shrug and changed the subject to the possibility of a blizzard in the next few days.

I hardly spoke. I just listened and watched and felt.

If we were in a play, Devin was the director and I was the chorus girl. But at least I had a part.

live for *me*

ATER ON THE DRIVE BACK to Devin's house, I got a text from Cat.

I'm not ok with this. He's a Chester the Molester.

It blindsided me. Wow. She wasn't holding back. I answered with a curt, *Why?*

You say all the time you look young. He's too old for his interest to be anything but creeper.

What hurt was I knew she was right in that I looked young. But I also knew that Devin wasn't attracted to me because of my appearance. He liked my mind, the way I stood up to him. The fact that when I spoke I didn't ramble endlessly about stupid shit. It was complicated. Attraction wasn't just about big tits.

She hadn't been there with us for the last few weeks. She hadn't heard the things he'd said to me.

Angry with her for throwing that out in a text, regardless of how worried about me she was, I didn't answer.

"Is everything okay?" Devin asked, pulling into the driveway at Richfield.

It was snowing and he took the turn too fast so that we fishtailed a bit. It was ridiculous to drive a sports car in Maine in December and he knew it. He'd been talking about buying an SUV in town and putting the Lamborghini in the garage for the rest of the winter. Almost like he intended to stay.

For some reason he refused to drive the truck that already sat in his garage. I wondered if it had something to do with Kadence.

I nodded in response to his question. "Just got a reminder that I'm on my own. That I'm alone." I didn't usually give in to feeling sorry for myself, but Cat's texts felt like a betrayal.

His hand stroked over my knee. "You're not alone. You have me."

chapter nine

EVIN'S WORDS MADE ME ANGRY. He didn't understand what it did to me. To him, it was a casual platitude. He meant it, I knew he did. In a way that someone did who has a ton of friends, family, wealth, privilege. He never had to be alone. Not truly and earnestly.

For me, it was a harsh reality. I was well and truly alone.

If I died tomorrow, maybe five people would show up at my funeral.

That wasn't self-pity, that was reality. I had been quiet in school, and unable to participate in extracurricular activities. My hope was that I could go to nursing school as planned, reach out and help people the way isolated foster parents had for me over the years. To be kind in a world where there was so little kindness. I had no lofty goals or expectations of wealth, travel, even love. Maybe someday I would find a guy who would get me and could tolerate that I had the Great Wall of China in front of my emotions.

That guy wasn't Devin, no matter how much I wanted it to be. Whatever love I felt for him, whatever feelings he might have for me, they were transient, temporary.

Ultimately, I was alone.

"Don't patronize me," I said, jerking my leg so his hand fell off my knee.

His jaw dropped. "I'm not. I'm telling you that I'm your friend." He parked the car in the garage and turned to me. "What, you don't believe me? After everything?"

"I believe that I am, for now." Not wanting to look at him, I stared out the window at his immaculate three-car garage. Everything was orderly, with a built-in storage system for the tools and equipment no one used. Sometimes it seemed to me like Richfield was a movie set, not a real house. Like at any minute cast and crew would stream in, pull off the sheets, pretend like there was life and vitality happening there, then retreat, leaving it silent and empty again.

"What is going on?" Devin asked, sounding frustrated. "Who texted you?"

But I didn't bother to answer because sitting on the work bench was that freaky Kadence doll. "Why is that doll in the garage?" I asked, curious and a little unnerved. I hated that doll. It was so... plastic. Sort of like its inspiration. But more to the point, I didn't understand why Devin would want that thing around.

"What? What are you talking about?"

I pointed. "That doll that was on your bed."

When I looked over at him, Devin was peering around me into the depths of the garage. "I don't see anything," he said flatly. "And I don't know what you're talking about. I don't have a doll on my bed."

"You don't?" That was weird.

"No. Why would I have a doll? That is not something I would choose to collect and it's a little bizarre that you think I would." With that, he opened his car door and got out.

I did the same. "That doll," I said, pointing to it. "It was on your bed."

Devin came around the car and frowned. "Oh, shit, that thing? I thought my ex-wife took that with her. It was designed to look like her." He picked it up and turned it over so that the blond hair flopped over her face. "I think it's hideous and weird, personally."

"It was on your bed," I insisted.

"When were you in my room?" he asked.

That wasn't the relevant part of my statement. "When you weren't here. Why does that matter?"

But he was smiling, that smug male smile that says he knows you were checking him out. He tossed the doll back down.

"Hey, come here, Tiff." He held his hand out for me.

I ignored it. "I think you should check the surveillance footage. Someone was in the house." I shivered at the thought that I hadn't been alone when Devin was back in New York. That someone had come in to the house without me knowing.

"Okay." He took my hand and pulled me up against him. "Don't worry about it. It's just an ugly doll."

"There was potentially an intruder."

live for *me*

"I'll take care of it. Don't worry. I don't want you to ever worry. You're not alone. I mean that."

I wasn't in the mood to listen to reassurances he thought I'd want to hear. So I just moved around him toward the house. "It's cold out here."

Going in through the back door, I bent down to greet Amelia. "If you want cookies for Christmas, I'm going to need to go to the store."

"Are you talking to the dog or to me?" Devin asked.

Smart ass. He sounded as annoyed as I felt.

"Unless the dog can drive I'm talking to you."

Devin moved past me into the kitchen. "By the way, I have something for you." He reached into the desk drawer and pulled out an envelope, which had already been opened. "Since you were never going to do it, I ordered your birth certificate for you. Now you can go and legally get your temps."

"You did?" I admit, I was surprised. I had been ignoring the issue because I still didn't really see the point in getting my driver's license. I didn't even have a car to take the test unless I used Devin's, which seemed ludicrous.

"Yes. And I thought you said you're eighteen."

"I am."

"According to your birth certificate, you're actually nineteen."

Um, that was not what I was expecting him to say. "What? That's not possible. Someone would have told me at some point. I was in foster care. Those things pop up."

"Well, apparently they're all fucking idiots because I can do math and that piece of paper clearly states you're nineteen."

Unfolding the birth certificate I'd withdrawn from the

envelope I studied all the data on it. He was right. The year was one earlier than my grandmother had always told me. What the hell? It also had something I'd never seen before- my father's name. Randy Hart.

He had a name. I liked the sound of it. I also liked that my mother had listed him on the birth certificate. Like it mattered. Like he mattered to her.

"Do you feel older and wiser?" he asked.

Just really confused. "But that means I started school a year late. This doesn't make any sense. I don't understand how it never came up with me."

"Maybe you could ask your grandmother about it. Maybe there was a reason."

"It doesn't matter, I guess." Though it felt like it mattered. I'd lost a year of my life without even being aware of it. And again, it felt like other people had controlled me, my fate, carelessly and without letting me in on it. "But it feels very weird. That means I only get to be nineteen for a few months."

"You're almost twenty." Devin sounded pleased by that fact. Like it relieved him of a certain burden of perversion.

That might be the only positive. It might encourage him to move a little faster with what we'd started. "Are you sure this is valid?"

"Of course." He kicked his shoes off by Amelia's dog bed, peeled off his jacket, and went to the refrigerator. "I want some wine and a fire in the fireplace. You want anything?"

I shook my head.

"I feel like I should have gotten you a Christmas tree since I'm stealing you from your friends."

That would have been nice, I had to admit. "It doesn't matter. I've only had a tree twice when I was with foster families."

"You say it doesn't matter a lot," he told me, head still buried in the shelves, looking for what I had no idea. He emerged with a block of Brie cheese. "I don't believe you."

"It is what it is. I'm not bitter."

"I know you're not. Which is one of the reasons I find you so amazing."

The doorbell rang. Damn it. Lousy, shitty timing. "I'll get it."

Devin let me, which surprised me. Usually he followed me when I went and did something. He was like a little kid or a dog that way- he didn't like to be left alone in rooms.

When I opened the front door, all I saw was greenery and a guy with a knit hat on his head. "Where should we put it?" he asked.

"Put what?" I asked stupidly.

"The tree."

"What tree?" Even though I could clearly see he was holding a Christmas tree in his hand.

"This tree. Look, this is Mr. Gold's house, right?"

"Yes." Realizing that Devin had been messing with me, that he had clearly ordered a Christmas tree, I opened the door wider and stepped back. "Sorry, come in. Devin," I called. "Where do you want the tree?"

He appeared in the foyer, looking pleased with himself. "By the fireplace, in front of the window." He gestured to his right for the guy.

A woman followed the man, carrying three plastic containers piled high in her arms. I raised an eyebrow at Devin.

"Ornaments," he said, like it should have been obvious.

"Right." I couldn't help but smile. He could be very thoughtful when he wanted to be. Even if he liked to tease.

"They're going to light the tree and decorate it for us."

And with that, the joy and sweetness of his surprise evaporated. "What? Oh, hell no. We're decorating it." Was he for real? "Get your hands dirty, G Daddy."

He made a face at me. "It will look better if someone else does it."

"And why do we care what it looks like if we're the only ones here? It's supposed to be special, not to sit as a perfect display. I've never gotten to decorate a tree." I wasn't going to stand there and watch someone get paid to do it. So weird.

Though probably no weirder than my role in Devin's life.

"Fine." He looked uncertain about the whole thing, but he helped the woman set the boxes down on the floor as the man put the tree into a stand.

Needles rained to the hardwood and the scent of pine filled the air. It felt completely bizarre to have two total strangers standing in the family room assembling a tree. I wanted them gone so I could stand back and appreciate having my own Christmas tree. Mine. Ours. Devin might have arranged it and paid for it, but it was *our* tree. Though I knew that had been his intention.

"Thank you," I told the guy as he stepped back to assess the position of the tree.

He smiled at me. He was in his forties. "You're welcome. I told your father you need a high ceiling for a fir tree like this one, but clearly this room fits the bill."

My father? Nice. That was the last thing Devin needed to hear someone say. It would just raise his doubts all over again. I managed a tight smile. "Yeah, it really does. It's going to be beautiful."

Devin either didn't hear or he was determined not to acknowledge what the guy said. He just signed some papers and escorted them both to the front door, which he slammed shut after them.

"I don't look like your father," he said, striding back into the room as I was taking a lid off one of the containers. He sounded more angry than embarrassed.

"No. You don't," I said calmly. "But I called you G Daddy. He just heard the 'daddy' part. You're older than me. Don't take it personally." People made assumptions. Enormous and erroneous ones. Like even my best friend, who couldn't believe that Devin's interest in me could be normal. To her it was deviant that he would like me, and that stung.

Even though I knew if the roles were reversed I would be saying the same thing. I wanted her to trust me. To trust that I knew Devin. That I knew what I was doing.

"So maybe you shouldn't call me Daddy anymore."

"No problem. It doesn't really feel right. It doesn't seem like you to me." I didn't want to make it a bigger issue than it should be, so I left it at that. I picked through the box. All the ornaments were natural materials, with a woodland theme. Very Maine.

"It is me," he said shortly.

Wow. He was in a charming mood. "Did you pick this theme?" I asked. "I love it."

"I wanted an owl theme." He leaned over the box and startled me by kissing me, a soft worshipful kiss. "They do remind me of you, like I told you. Wise and always watching."

Both the kiss and the compliment loosened me up. It felt so natural, so easy for him to kiss me. I smiled up at him. "Thanks. This was very sweet of you."

"I have my moments." He tapped my arm. "Take your coat off. Stay awhile."

"I'd love to." Those words had more weight than I intended. I was on my knees on the rug. He was bent over and at my words his movements were arrested.

Devin ran a finger down over my cheek. "Good," he said, roughly.

He moved over to survey the tree.

"So how do we do this?" I asked, taking my hat and jacket off. I lifted a fluffy white owl ornament out of the box.

"You could look it up online," he said, teasing. "Or you could just put ornaments wherever you want and see what happens."

"You're very funny." The tree was already lit, plugged in by Tree Guy. The soft white lights glowed in the dark room.

"I know." He bent over, snagged a pinecone ornament and put it in some random spot.

I followed his example and in twenty minutes we had a beautiful Christmas tree. It wouldn't win any awards, but it had reindeer, owls, raccoons, and even a moose on it, all looking out at me in cute adoration. I felt like Snow White surrounded by my critters. "I love it," I told him. "It's perfect."

"It looks a little lopsided, but I'm glad you like it. I need another glass of wine. You want anything?"

I shook my head, and sat down on the couch just to stare at

the tree in wonder. My tree. Our tree. Gratitude and love were all jumbling together and making me more open and vulnerable than I'd been in a long time. I suspected my heart was in my eyes when Devin returned, not just with a glass of wine, but with a present in his hand.

"I was going to wait, but I don't exactly have a lot of patience," he said, handing it to me.

It was gold foil, with a red bow on top. "What is this?"

"A present, you silly woman."

"I know that. But what is it?" It was a stupid question, but I was so in awe of the perfection of the package in my hand, and the sentiment behind it, I wasn't sure what to do or say. We'd been moving towards something more, something intense and real, but this was different.

This was a gift. For me.

"So… I asked myself what would Tiffany want? And then I realized that you don't *want* anything. You think in terms of what you need. So I thought maybe you needed this." He unplucked the ribbon on top, clearly impatient with my pace. "Open it."

I swallowed hard, suddenly afraid. What would Devin think I needed?

Popping the lid off, I had my answer. It was a set of car keys on a turquoise blue keychain with Tiffany and Co embossed on it.

"It's Tiffany blue," he said, reaching in and pulling the keys out and holding them up for me. "And so is the jeep. I had to pull some strings to get the color done so quickly, but it turned out really well. It will be here by next week."

I stared at the keys as they dangled in front of me, brand

new. Silver. Shiny. The leather strap of the keychain elegant. Expensive. Together, they belonged to a car. Which Devin was saying belonged to me. A jeep. That he had thought to get, to pay for, to give to me.

"For the long winters, a jeep is perfect," he added.

"You bought me a jeep?" I asked, throat tight. My voice didn't sound like me. I sounded husky and raw and far away.

I could count on one hand the number of times I'd received a present and each one had been special. I could describe each one in great detail. How old I'd been, where I'd been given the gift, what it had been. To the teddy bear at five, to the sweater at eight, to the coffee mug at fifteen. But this… this was incomprehensible. This was beyond a gift. This was huge.

The tears in my eyes blurred my view of him and I blinked, hard, not wanting to cry. "Why would you do that?" I asked.

Devin's hand cupped my cheek. "Because, Tiffany Ennis, I find myself in the very uncomfortable position of having feelings for you that I don't fully understand or welcome. It doesn't seem like the person who has my heart in a vice should be a decade younger than me and even more solemn than me. But I've never met anyone like you, never met anyone I admired so much. I just wanted to give you something to show you that I appreciate who you are."

I didn't how what to say. Wasn't sure I could speak. He was saying that he loved me. Between the lines, that was precisely what he was saying. That he didn't want to, that he didn't understand it, but that I was in his heart. The way he was in mine. I wasn't sure that I could accept the enormity of his gift, if I could live with myself for taking something so expensive, knowing our relationship was never going to last.

But at that moment, I didn't care. I didn't care about anything but Devin and the way his eyes shone with affection and desire. I only cared that he had thought about me, had made phone calls and arrangements on my behalf. That I occupied space in his crowded brain. That the girl who'd spent her whole life on a rock in the middle of the ocean might matter to him.

"I don't know how to say thank you," I whispered. "It's a very big gift."

"You could just say thank you."

"Thank you," I murmured, wrapping my hand around his to clasp the keys. I leaned in, let my lips drift apart in invitation. I wanted him to kiss me. I wanted him.

"You're welcome." He kissed me softly. "It was my pleasure."

I tried to tell myself that to Devin, the price of a car affected his bottom line the way a latte might affect mine. It wasn't that big of a deal to him. But it was. I could see it in his eyes. In the way his hand shook slightly as he drew his thumb across my bottom lip. "Is this what you want?" he asked before kissing me deeper, his tongue teasing mine. "Really?"

The question was ludicrous. When he released me, I nodded. "Yes. It's all I want."

Devin took the gift box I was still holding and threw it on the floor. It tumbled a foot with a clatter that seemed loud in the quiet of the family room. But before I could comment, he did the same with the keys we were holding together. His eyes were stormy as he gathered me into his arms, his hands possessive and greedy more than gentle. The strength of his hold lifted me up off my feet onto the tips of my toes as he crushed me in a series of kisses that left me breathless, panting.

I clung to his shoulders and reveled that this was really happening. Devin was kissing me with fervor and passion and I was pretty damn sure a little bit of love. If not love, than a heady emotion that wasn't too far away from it. When I had been kissed by my first love interest at fifteen, it had been wet and fumbling and I had kept trying, wondering when it was going to feel good, wondering if every girl out there was in fact faking her reaction to a guy. At seventeen it had been better, but what I did in the dark to myself was entirely different than what he did, and I found with guilt that I preferred flying solo.

With Devin all those experiences were eradicated. They were nothing. In fact, they'd never existed. There was no guy before Devin, not any that mattered. With my first kiss from him that morning, a new chapter of my sexuality had been started, and he inked another word with each touch, caress, kiss.

"The way you look at me," he murmured. "It's... powerful."

I felt powerful and weak and overwhelmed all at once. I touched his cheek, enjoying the stimulation of his beard stubble on my fingertips. Every inch of me felt alive, electric. Eyes still trained on him, I took his hand and laced my fingers through his. Bringing our fists up together, I kissed his knuckles, one by one. "This *is* powerful. You and me."

He made a sound in the back of his throat, then he buried his lips in my neck and kissed down my clavicle bone, tugging at my shirt with his fingers to free my skin to his touch. My eyes drifted shut as I gave in to him, head falling back. While his lips moved across my neck, his hands shifted under my shirt, finding their way up to my breasts, where he brushed across my nipples with a light, deft touch. Then he was guiding me down and before I even understood how it had happened, I was on my back on the couch, sweater off over my head.

Devin was touching me everywhere and I had no hesitation, no modesty, no embarrassment. All that mattered was him, and the hot, wet desire he was coaxing to life with his hands, his mouth, his hips lightly thrusting against me, our jeans rustling. I could feel his erection here and there, when he pushed against me, or brushed my leg, and I wanted more on an instinctive level. That deep urgent ache swelled tremulously inside me, desperate for completion. As he teased and sucked my nipple through the cotton of my bra, I spread my legs, wanting him closer, locking my ankles behind his. It felt right, easy, languid. I panted and moaned, rolling my hips when his hand cupped my sex. Pausing only to remove his shirt, he kissed me down there through my jeans and I shifted, restless, surprised at how good it felt.

Sensation flooding me, thoughts jumbled and chaotic, I undid the button on my jeans myself. He looked up at me over the length of my body, his expression fierce. I closed my eyes for a split second, not sure how to say what I wanted. Not even really sure what I wanted. Truthfully, I wanted him to show me what I needed.

"Please," I whispered.

Tenderness came over his face. I'd never seen that expression from him, and I almost told him to stop, afraid it was too much. That I was in over my head. Devin Gold being sexy was one thing. Devin looking sweet and loving was more than I could handle. But before I could speak, he had my jeans down at my ankles. Cool air brushed over my skin and I lay in shock at how suddenly naked I was, physically and emotionally. He'd taken my panties with my jeans and there was nothing protecting me from his view. I inwardly cringed at how exposed I felt, at how I was nothing like socialites in New York.

"I don't wax," I said, which was stupid, because he could clearly see that. There was no point in me grooming any more than a tidying of the bikini line. It had always seemed like a colossal waste of time.

His fingers were massaging below my bellybutton, right over my pubic bone, distracting me from my anxiety. He was so close to where he should be, but so far away. And he knew it.

"I prefer you natural. Nothing else would suit you." He kissed one hipbone, then the other.

One finger sank into my moist heat and I sucked in my breath. Then before I could protest or beg he covered me with his tongue.

I'd never felt that before, and the raw intimacy, the shivering, shuttering ecstasy, had me clamping my legs together, trapping his head between my thighs. Devin maneuvered himself further in, his hair tickling my bare skin, his arm shoving my left leg down onto the couch cushion, pinning it. He licked, he kissed, he sucked at me, and I squeezed my eyes shut, assaulted by sensation. I'd never felt anything so intense, so deep and wet and delicious. An orgasm rushed me, catching me completely off guard as it consumed my whole body with pleasure.

"Oh, my God," I blurted, not caring that it was cliché. There was no other way to describe what the fucking hell was happening to me.

He kept at me until I finally stopped shuddering. When he

lifted his head, wiping his mouth, a smug expression on his face, I blushed. A full on middle school blush. My legs were spread on either side of his head and my jeans were caught at my ankles. My bra was still on, but it was completely crooked, nipples uncovered. Overwhelmed, I looked away toward the Christmas tree. Amelia was sitting on the area rug on her butt watching us.

"Oh, my God, the dog is watching us." That to me was more embarrassing than anything else.

"What?" Devin glanced over, kissing my inner thigh before sitting up. He gave a crack of laughter. "She looks offended."

Amelia barked. My cell phone started buzzing in the pocket of my jeans, dangling over the side of the couch. I clamped my legs together and rolled on my side, self-conscious of what Devin was seeing.

"You don't have to hide from the dog," he said, casually resting his hand on my bare hip. "I'm pretty sure she's okay with it. Or if you want, we can go upstairs and shut the door."

Go into his bedroom? Shut and lock the door? I wanted to. I really, really did. But now, lying there awkwardly, I was scared. I had no idea what I was doing. Look at what had just happened. He'd gotten me off and yet was still wearing pants. I'd yet to touch or see his penis. Nervous that I had no clue how to satisfy him, I felt like I should warn him so he'd know what he was getting. Which was me very much willing, but also totally and completely clueless.

I could have said or explained any of that. He probably knew I was a virgin anyway and had adjusted his expectations.

Instead I just blurted out, "I'm a virgin."

Because that's what every guy wants to hear when clothes

have already come off.

His hand had made inroads into my thighs again, and his thumb was stroking over my sensitive and swollen clitoris, but he froze at my words.

"What?"

"I'm a virgin," I repeated. "I thought you should know." Lamest. Sentence. Ever.

I bit my lip, crossing my legs without even realizing I was going to. The movement trapped his hand between my thighs. His Adam's apple shifted as he swallowed hard.

"I-

Then he shook his head, like he'd changed his mind about whatever he'd intended to say. Extracting his hand he reached for his wine glass on the floor, but it was empty. "I need a drink." Sitting back, he took a deep breath, like he was steadying himself, then stood and went toward the kitchen, glass in hand. His jeans were resting low on his hips, his feet bare, the muscles of his back flexing as he rolled his neck, like he needed to work out some tension.

I watched him, heart racing. Wow. I had completely and totally screwed that up.

Unable to just lie there mostly naked, I yanked my panties up first, then kicked my jeans completely off, so I could turn them right side in and put them back on. My phone was buzzing again, so I retrieved it from the pocket and checked it. I had five texts. The first two were apologies from Cat. The next asked me to call her. It was the fourth one that made me sit up.

Your grandma is in the hospital. She wants to see you.

The last text had the information of where she was staying. It was on the mainland about twenty minutes from Richfield.

My hand was shaking as I answered Cat.

What happened?

I don't know. But the neighbors called me looking for you.

Ok, thanks.

Let me know if you need me to do anything.

Dropping my phone for a second, I fixed my bra and pulled my sweater back on.

Devin came back into the room, sipping from the glass in his right hand, the whole bottle in his left. It seemed it was a Merlot moment. He eyed my movements as I slipped my feet into the legs of my jeans.

"Are we done?"

It sounded rude. It was rude. I lifted my butt up and yanked them the rest of the way. "That was my impression since you left the room."

"I was thirsty."

"You were horrified," I shot back.

"I was caught off guard. You could have shared that little piece of information sooner."

"When is a good time to tell someone that?" I asked, annoyed. So I was a virgin. What the hell did he expect? As he kept pointing out to me, I was an infant. In fact, I actually felt like I might cry. I searched the floor for the shoes I'd kicked off. "When you kissed me? Over dinner last week? Should I have put it on my job application?"

"Don't be a brat, it doesn't suit you," he said. "I went in the kitchen to absorb what you just told me. Don't act like I hired you thinking I could nail you. I wasn't even here."

"You're right." I stood up, shoes on and went for my coat. "You were in the city fucking Amazing Abs Brooke. I'm sorry if it unnerves you that I haven't been fucking someone too." It felt nasty and mean to be swearing at him, but I couldn't stop myself. I was worried about my grandmother, and I was pissed at him for abandoning me in the midst of my confession. It was hard for me to share what was going on inside, and I had needed his reassurance, not his horror.

I'd already shared so much of myself with him that maybe giving everything was more frightening that I expected. Maybe I was terrified of rejection and this felt pretty damn close to rejection.

He paused in the middle of tossing back the rest of the liquid in his glass. "I expect better from you than crazy."

The words shamed me. He was right. I was being childish. "If I knew what I was doing, I wouldn't be a virgin. And how could you not know anyway? It seems implied to me."

Devin sighed. He put the bottle down on the end table. "I didn't even think about it one way or the other. It's been a long time since I encountered a virgin."

Well. "So I'm a dying breed?"

"You're young," he shot back. "A fact I'm both keenly aware of and repeatedly try to ignore. But I'm glad you told me. We can slow it down. I don't want to do something you'll regret." Then he gave me a rueful smile. "I don't want to do something I'll regret. Maybe this isn't the right thing for us, right now. Maybe we need to retreat a bit."

He didn't mean it the way it sounded. I didn't think. But it felt like a second rejection and I felt like an idiot. I couldn't look at him knowing he'd seen me naked, knowing the sounds I had made, the places his tongue had been.

"I need to go. My grandmother is in the hospital."

"What?" He looked at me blankly.

"My grandmother is in the hospital. Cat just texted me. I need to go see her."

"Why? She hasn't spoken to you in what, three months?"

"She asked to see me," I said simply.

"So? She treated you like shit, Tiffany. You don't owe her anything."

I knew that. But he couldn't understand and I didn't expect him to understand. His family had been loving, supportive, and he took that for granted. A part of me would always crave my grandmother's affection, approval. Need wasn't the same as love, but that she thought of me when she was ill mattered. Besides, if I turned my back on her, if I said screw it, and gave in to anger, detachment, than how was I any better than her? I wanted to be a good person, compassionate, regardless of what was said or done to me. That was the standard I held for myself, the way I'd managed to survive all those years. I wouldn't give in to hatred.

"I know I don't owe her anything. But she's the only family I have. If she wants to see me, I need to go."

Devin studied me for a second, than shook his head. "All right. Do what you need to do. Where is she? I'll drive you there."

"Thank you." There was a pit in my stomach as he put his shirt on, then sat on the couch and pulled his socks over his feet.

I was worried about my grandmother. How would I feel if she died? What if I couldn't see her first? I pictured her face, the frown she always gave me. It didn't seem possible that someone so filled with negative emotion would ever find peace, yet I wanted that for her. I hoped this was just a scare that would show her she needed to appreciate her life. That it would allow her to live better.

For the first time since Devin had gotten back to Richfield I felt uncomfortable around him. His movements were purposeful, arrogant. He didn't comfort me. He didn't reach for me. He didn't hold me and stroke my hair and tell me everything would be okay. The tenderness he'd shown briefly had evaporated with my pronouncement and I knew him well enough to know what he was thinking- he didn't want to deal with a virgin. He knew it would mean too much to me. He knew I would attach.

So he was detaching.

I couldn't blame him. But that didn't mean it didn't hurt.

All the reasons he had hesitated, all the weeks he'd been fighting his feelings, and now his fears were realized. I was too young.

The house felt quiet, empty, as he grabbed his coat and took one last sip of his wine. He wasn't speaking. I wasn't speaking.

Bending over, I retrieved the Tiffany keychain with the car keys jingling on it and held it tightly before putting it inside my coat pocket and zipping it shut. He'd been so happy to give me a present and I felt that somehow I'd ruined it.

His phone rang. He answered it without apologizing to me like he usually did. "Hello?"

I followed behind him, giving Amelia a rub on the head as we went past her into the garage. The garage was heated, but I still shivered. A storm was definitely brewing. When Devin opened the garage door a wicked wind rushed in.

"Plans have changed," he said to whoever it was. "I'll keep you posted. Thanks."

He tucked his phone back away in his pocket. He opened the car door for me. I got in. He shut it.

Then we pulled out of the garage and away from Richfield.

I saw the Christmas tree lit up in front of the family room window and I suddenly wondered if I was ever coming back.

chapter ten

GRANDMA LOOKED LIKE HELL. SHE had lost weight and she lay against the hospital bed pale and vapid. Even when her eyes opened and focused on me, there was no spark, no recognition.

My throat closed up and I moved carefully towards her, reaching out to touch her hand. "Hi, Gram."

She pulled her hand out of my reach and gave me a petulant look. Oddly, it was reassuring. "What are you doing here?"

"Cat said you wanted to see me."

For a second, she didn't respond, her eyes closed. Then she said, "I need you to go clean the house. They say I'm going to be here for a spell."

Sure, Cinderella could sweep the fireplace. I didn't have it in me to argue with her. The doctors had told me it was unlikely she'd be coming home. She had stage four lung cancer and it was a miracle she was even speaking given the amount of pain killers they had her on. "Okay. Of course."

"So where have you been?" she asked. "Is it true you're some rich guy's mistress? That's what everyone is saying."

My eyes widened and I felt my cheeks burn. It had never occurred to me that anyone in Vinalhaven would talk about Devin and me. Maybe going to the coffee shop had started gossip. "I am not a rich guy's mistress. I'm a housesitter."

"Who brought you here?"

So she was determined to shame me. I raised my chin. I wasn't going to feel guilty. Devin and I had a *relationship*. "The owner."

She snorted. "Of course. If you haven't spread your legs yet you will soon enough. Just like your mother."

Despite the fact that I could still feel moisture between my legs from the arousal Devin had stoked to life an hour earlier, I wasn't going to give her the satisfaction of feeling dirty. My feelings for him were real. "Whatever issue you had with my mother, I think it's time for you to leave me out of it."

"I lied to your father, you know," she said suddenly, raising her hand to adjust the tubing in her nose, her breathing labored. "When he came looking for you."

That made me grip the bedrail tightly, my shoulders stiffening. "What are you talking about?"

"He came when you were eight, and in foster care. I guess he'd run into an old friend who told him your mother had a baby. He never knew you existed." She gave a weak cough. "I told him you died in a car accident. Even sent him to the cemetery where your mother is." She glared at me in defiance, breathing labored.

"Go ahead. Tell me I'm evil. But he had no business being part of your life."

I was having trouble breathing myself. My father wanted to see me? He had looked for me? It was the best news I could have ever hoped for. Yet I couldn't understand how my grandmother could be so cruel as to keep him from me. Me from him. He must have suffered thinking he'd had and lost a child and never once laid eyes on me. Tears filled my eyes. So much hatred for no reason that I could see.

I didn't want to perpetuate that kind of anger.

"It's in the past," I said. "I forgive you."

"I'm not asking for your forgiveness." Then she started wheezing so hard, it scared me. It sounded like she couldn't pull any air into her lungs.

I pushed the nurse call button, who appeared and shooed me out of the room.

In the hallway, I wandered down to the waiting area, where Devin was sitting on a hard plastic chair, looking at his phone. He glanced up. "Hey. She doing okay?"

"No. She's only got a few weeks at the most." I wasn't sure how to tell him what I had to say. "Cat is meeting me here. I'm going to go home for a few days to clean up my grandmother's house." She was going to die. Not even spite could keep her alive. I felt numb, but I also knew I wanted to go back to that house, the site of so much misery and boredom. The walls of my emotional confinement. I needed closure. I wanted to move on.

"Are you kidding me? Why would you do that?"

"Because I need to."

Tossing his hair out of his eyes he opened his mouth, then

closed it again. I appreciated the restraint. Devin stood up and finally, he gave me the hug I needed. His arms enclosed me and I leaned against his chest, closing my eyes, breathing in his cologne.

"Can I do anything? Do you need help? I can come with you."

The thought of Devin at my grandmother's was horrifying and comical. In fact, the image of him standing in her cluttered and tired living room was a slap in the face. He didn't belong in my world. I didn't belong in his.

"No, that's okay, but thank you." I looked up at him, studying his jawline, his lips, his strong nose. His dark and expressive eyes. "I appreciate everything you've done for me."

Devin had made me feel desirable. He'd made me feel that somewhere, there was a place for me in the world. A home. That I had words, thoughts, love, to contribute.

He frowned, his hands tightening on my back. "Why does that sound like goodbye? You're coming back aren't you?"

I nodded. I would, because I had nowhere else to go. But I wasn't sure that I could stay.

He shook me a little. "Promise me. We have unfinished business."

Whatever that meant. But I couldn't say no to him. "I promise. I'll be back. I'll keep in touch."

*B*UT I DIDN'T, NOT REALLY. Because on Christmas day my grandmother died in the hospital while I held her hand. Her labored breathing ceased and the machines pumping who knew what into her all flatlined, a horrible continuous chirp coming from one of them. I could smell death in the room and it filled my nostrils, made me swallow over and over. One minute there was life, a straining, rotting, struggle for existence, the next it was gone. The room was empty.

A nurse appeared and said things. Things I didn't remember two seconds after she spoke them as I stared blankly at my grandmother. Her eyes were closed and I felt... nothing. And everything.

My phone beeped with a text from Devin.

Merry Christmas. Xxx

Hugs, but not kisses. I stared at the screen for a second, not sure what to do. The nurse clasped my hand, led me into the hallway. There were Christmas lights twinkling above the nurses' station and the staff was all wearing Santa caps. A tree was in the corner with red and gold balls hanging on it. I stood in the hallway, looking back over my shoulder at the room where my grandmother lay.

Another nurse came up to me and put her arm around my shoulders. "Is there someone you want to call, hon?"

I shook my head. There was no one to call. It had always just been me and my grandmother. "No."

There was no ferry to the island at night, so I slept on the chairs in the waiting room, my coat spread over me.

I woke up under the bright lights with Christmas music blaring around me, someone laughing down the hall.

It smelled like antiseptic and I closed my eyes again. Alone.

*S*ITTING IN *C*AT'S *LIVING ROOM,* I stared at nothing. "I have to go back," I told her. To Richfield. I didn't really want to, though I wasn't entirely sure why. Maybe I just didn't know what to say to Devin. I didn't want him to look at me and feel sorry for me. That I had been mistreated as a kid. That my grandmother was dead. To see that he didn't want a relationship with me after all, because of my lack of sexual and life experience. That friendship and desire would devolve into pity.

So mostly I wanted to drink coffee at Cat and Heath's and read one book after another. I didn't want to do anything and I didn't want to even respond to Devin, whose texts to me were getting increasingly agitated. He'd even called me twice. I hadn't answered any of them, which was awful and immature. I knew that. But I couldn't deal with him, not when I was dealing with my grandmother's death. I didn't want to admit I'd allowed expectations to grow beyond what they ever should have.

"No, you don't," Cat told me. She was lacing up her running shoes. The promised blizzard hadn't arrived and there was only the usual soft December snow on the ground. She didn't let that prevent her from jogging. Heath was outside already splitting wood. "You can stay here. Your grandmother's house is yours, you know. It's a shithole, but it's your shithole. You can do online classes like you originally planned."

"I promised him I'd go back."

She opened her mouth. Then she just bit her lip and stood, pulling on a knit cap and mittens.

"You don't think he'll care, do you?" I asked. I was wearing sweatpants and I plucked at the loose fabric. "It's the right thing to do, regardless."

"So go back and resign or whatever. He wasn't here for you when your grandmother died. You don't need that kind of guy in your life."

148

"I didn't tell him."

"What?" She stared at me.

"I didn't tell him she died. It's been five days and I haven't told him."

"Why not?" she asked, clearly astonished.

"I don't know." I didn't. Maybe it had something to do with me not wanting to have either his pity or his disinterest. I was afraid of his response. I didn't trust that he would give me the one I needed.

It wasn't fair to him, truthfully.

And he was clearly worried about me. But I couldn't unstick my tongue from the roof of my mouth. All of this only served to illuminate how different our worlds, our lives, were from each other.

There wasn't going to be a funeral. My grandmother had already been cremated and she was in a box in a grocery bag I'd taken from the house. I had locked everything up and left it with the heat turned down, doubtful that I could ever bring myself to live there. I wasn't sure how all the legal stuff worked but hopefully I could pay back the funeral home and ditch the house somehow. There wasn't even anything I wanted in it.

The only thing I'd taken was the pot holder I'd made. I'd found it in the trunk in my grandmother's bedroom, along with pictures of my mother growing up.

"I wish you would let people help you," Cat said. "I mean, whatever Devin is doing, he clearly does care about you."

I raised an eyebrow. "I thought you said he is playing me."

She pursed her lips. "He brought you to the hospital. He's been blowing up your phone. He clearly cares."

live for *me*

"Yeah." My grandmother's words echoed in my head. Rich man's mistress. The keys to the jeep he'd bought me were still in my coat pocket.

That's not the way he had intended it. I knew Devin. He would have given me the jeep regardless. He'd actually ordered it before we'd even shared our first kiss. It wasn't a manipulation. He could get pussy whenever and wherever he wanted it. With a lot less work and a much more satisfying outcome for him. With women who knew what they were doing. He also wasn't the kind who manipulated others just to see if he could get his way. He just wanted me, for whatever reason.

I thought about the simple pleasure on his face when he'd given me the box. How eager he'd been.

Pulling my phone out I sent him a text.

Hope you had a good Christmas. Can you pick me up at the ferry dock? I'm ready to come back to Richfield. Sorry it was longer than I thought.

That wasn't good enough. I knew it wasn't. Not after going dead silent on him for five days.

Which was obvious when he texted back.

I thought you fell in the ocean. Yes. When?

Tomorrow? Any time you're free. Thank you.

"I wonder if he went to New York," I mused out loud. "If he stayed at the house by himself for Christmas, I really am a total jerk."

"Your grandmother died, Tiffany, I think he'll understand."

I hoped so.

I hoped he would understand that this was a path I'd had to follow alone. That our new and fragile relationship, whatever it was exactly, needed to be separate from something as emotional and overwhelming as death. That I'd been unable to trust him.

Or trust myself not to want something he could never give me. Love. A home. Family. Forever. That was what I wanted.

If I had the courage, that was what I would ask for.

*U*NFORTUNATELY, WHAT I WASN'T EXPECTING was Devin to pick me up at the ferry dock with two total strangers in the back seat of his car. I had been standing there for about twenty minutes talking to Marty, the ferry operator, who had been friends with Cat's brother back in high school. Or Martin, as he told me he now preferred to be called.

"Who the hell is that?" Martin asked when the Lamborghini tore into the parking lot faster than was necessary, music blaring audibly even with all the windows closed. It was a driving R&B beat.

"That's my boss." I picked up the bag at my feet and gave Martin a smile. "Thanks for keeping me company."

"Are you sure you should go with that guy?" Martin adjusted the hat on his head and frowned in Devin's direction.

He was out of the car now, the music louder. He strode toward me, and I started walking fast, not wanting to introduce them. I could see people in the backseat of the car. Devin looked sulky. I suspected I was going to be punished with bad behavior for my silence. I probably deserved it. I just wished it didn't mean I had to talk to strangers.

"Hey." He reached out and took the bag from my hand. "How is your grandmother? Doing better?"

I shook my head.

151

"No? I'm sorry." In five steps we were back at the car and I didn't want to elaborate. "I hope you don't mind, but I was already picking up Jay and Sapphire at the train station."

"Um… no, of course not." I peered into the backseat as we got to the car, trying not to be obvious. "Is that the singer Sapphire?"

"Yep. And her husband, who is a DJ. Jay Ray. Heard of him?"

Unless I lived under a rock, yes, I had heard of them. Of both of them. "Are they staying at the house?" I was seriously regretting my decision to go back to Richfield.

"New Year's Eve party. There are three other couples already at the house."

Fabulous. Wonderful. Not. I felt a little sick to my stomach. "I'm sorry, I didn't meant to interrupt…"

"Don't piss me off," he said, opening the passenger door for me. "I'm already seriously annoyed with you. You couldn't at least text me and let me know you were okay? I was fucking worried about you!"

"I'm sorry. It was emotional." Then I slipped into the car before he could question me further. I turned to the backseat, feeling small and ordinary. "Hi. I'm sorry you had to come out of your way to pick me up."

"Not a problem," Sapphire said, and her smile looked genuine enough.

She was a platinum blonde with a skin tone similar to mine, her eyes heavily made up with blue shadow. She was wearing a cashmere hat and a leather jacket. The guy, wearing a camel colored trench coat, didn't even look at me.

"Let's get this party started," Devin said, jumping in and putting the car in drive.

He didn't sound like my Devin. He sounded fake. Falsely enthusiastic. "Who wants the first shot of Crown?"

"Oh, God, seriously, G?" Sapphire asked. "You're such a white boy."

Jay Ray laughed and I saw he had a gold grill on his front teeth.

Yeah. I was so out of my element.

Fortunately, or unfortunately, no one spoke to me. They taunted each other over drinking for a few minutes, then the conversation turned to people I'd never heard of who were in Vail for the week, and how maybe they all should go there once the ball dropped. They could fly west and celebrate midnight on New Year's all over again.

"We can celebrate it in three fucking time zones!" Jay Ray said.

"Let's do it." Devin pulled into his garage, parked, and turned around. "I'll text my assistant and have her set everything up."

I sat there, painfully awkward, my shopping bag with my grandmother's ashes at my feet. When we went into the house, I bent down and greeted Amelia, grateful for a familiar face. Grateful to be able to hide mine. There were voices coming from the family room, the kitchen. Laughter. Music. I moved as quickly as possible without attracting any attention, intending to head straight to my room.

"Where are you going?" Devin asked, cutting my escape off. He looked volatile, angry.

"To my room."

"Why?"

"Because these are your friends and you're having a party. I don't want to intrude."

"I want you here."

God, why was he doing this? Couldn't he see how uncomfortable I was? "Why?" Not one of these people would give two shits if I were there or not. Already I could see Sapphire darting curious glances back at us. A woman with an afro, the woman in one of the pictures in that packet that had been delivered, glanced around Sapphire at us as well. They whispered to each other.

I shuffled my weight from one foot to the other, miserable. I should have stayed at Cat's. That was clear.

"Because I want you here. I'm not asking," he added, taking the bag from my hand and setting it down on the console table by the garage door. "Now come and meet everyone."

Except that no one was particularly interested in meeting me. They all briefly glanced at me then went back to their conversations, their elaborate cocktails, their posturing. The women were tall and thin, except for Sapphire, who had bangin' curves and was tiny, maybe five feet tall. They talked about people in the music industry with affection or cattiness or disdain depending on the subject of gossip. They talked about the future of touring and digital downloads. They did shots and fiddled with their extensive jewelry and walked confidently on thousand dollar high heels.

The men swatted their asses from time to time, or gave affectionate kisses, but they too talked business and did shots, and smoked cigars in their expensive sweaters and jackets and Italian shoes. They were a mix of ethnicities and everyone was beautiful.

I sat in the corner by the Christmas tree and watched, saying nothing. The nine of them mingled, some in the kitchen, some near me, eating little appetizer things and completely ignoring me. At one point, two of the women made tidy lines of coke on the coffee table and sucked it up into their nostrils with diamond encrusted straws. Specialty drug paraphernalia. How Hollywood. Slap a diamond on everything you own.

Devin may or may not have been drunk, I wasn't really sure. He was louder than I was used to, clapping the other guys on their backs and showing off his surround sound stereo system. "It's all controlled from my phone or an iPad," he said, showing Jay Ray his phone. Suddenly the music shot up about ten notches.

"Turn that the fuck down!" the woman named Lizzie said. "I'm trying to talk."

She was giving me the poorest impression of all the guests. She had porcelain white skin, deep burgundy lips, and a halo of honey-colored curls around her face. Her features were delicate, doll-like, and she was dressed too young for her age, in tiny denim overalls that barely covered her ass, and socks that came up to her knees. But with boots that had six-inch heels and nothing but a bra. It was like pedophile porn star, but with a shitty attitude. Most of the night Lizzie had been scowling or giving an obnoxiously fake tinkling laugh. On two occasions she had met my eye and given me a smug smirk one time, a cold dismissal the other. Her boyfriend was a model who seemed determined to insert his hand up her overalls. She would swat at him without even breaking conversation with Sapphire.

"So why didn't you bring Brooke?" Lizzie called loudly in the direction of Devin.

live for *me*

I was sitting in my chair, legs tightly crossed, shoulders tense, and at that, I wished the cushion would open up and swallow me. I'd been trying to figure out how to slip out of the room unnoticed. I'd been hoping Devin would take the guys upstairs to his studio in the next stop on his Bragging Tour. But now Lizzie had brought him to the attention of everyone.

And where was Brooke? I admit I wanted to know myself. He'd never said he wasn't seeing her anymore. He'd admitted she was just a fuck buddy and of course, I knew he couldn't have seen her while he was at Richfield with me, but had he ever told Brooke they were done? Had he seen her since I'd been gone?

"Who's Brooke?" Devin asked.

Everyone laughed.

"I thought you were all right and tight with her," one of the guys said. "She's a foxy lady."

"It was just a casual thing," Devin said, waving his hand. "I haven't talked to her in a month."

I let out a sigh of relief. It would make me feel like shit if he were still involved with Brooke in any way. That was a line in the sand I wasn't willing to cross. I didn't want to be involved with a guy who was involved with someone else. Not that I was sure if Devin and I were actually still involved or not. But I hoped we were, despite my defection.

But the sound I made was too loud. Lizzie swiveled her head and narrowed her eyes at me.

Shit. I knew that look. It was the look foster siblings gave before they blamed something on me. I dropped my foot to the floor, anticipating something bad was about to go down. She was going to call attention to me, embarrass me. Ask if Devin and I were a thing.

But what she did was way worse.

With a smile, she said, "So when is your divorce going to be final, G? You need to negotiate custody of your friends better. Kadence had the balls to ask me to Turks and Caicos with her in a few weeks."

His divorce wasn't final? I dug my nails into my thigh, trying to steady myself, waiting for his response. I'd assumed they were divorced legally. Assumed. I realized that while he had frequently referred to Kadence as his ex-wife, he had never said anything about when their divorce was final. I had never researched it, not considering the possibility they were still married.

"Probably never," he said. "At first she was fighting me about everything. Down to the last fucking satin sheet. But now she's just refusing to participate in any negotiations." He raised his wine glass. "Fortunately it's done in two years whether she agrees to sign anything or not, court mandated. So I propose a toast. To lawyers. And their complete fucking inability to do their job while taking piles of money."

There was laughter all around.

Except from me. I felt like hyperventilating. I felt sick. Not only was he still married, he had completely failed to mention that he was in the midst of a divorce battle. The pictures delivered to the house suddenly made sense.

Liar. Cheater. Manwhore.

Brooke, the woman here at the party with the gorgeous afro, me. His conquests, lovers, whatever you wanted to call us. Women he fucked.

While still married.

live for *me*

I suddenly realized that I didn't know jack shit about anything, and I had been nothing but a complete little girl moron, swept away by some fantasy of friendship and love. Without any thought for what anyone would think, I jumped out of my chair and walked across the room, as close to the windows as I could cling. I had to get out. Get away.

"Tiffany!" he called after me.

I wasn't turning around. Nothing could make me turn back. I couldn't let those people, those rich and privileged and smug people, see that I was hurt. But at the last second, I veered toward the garage, wanting my bag off the console. I couldn't leave Gran there. But it was a miscalculation. When I turned, bag in hand, Devin was there, frowning.

"Where are you going?"

"To bed."

He tried to take my arm, but I jerked back. Amelia had followed me, and she barked at him in warning. The look he gave us both was thunderous. As I moved past him, he stepped in my path, so that we knocked shoulders. I dropped the bag, my trembling hands losing their grip. The box tumbled out, and opened slightly, so that ashes spilled onto the hardwood floor.

Oh, my God. With a cry of dismay, I dropped to my knees and righted the box so no more would fall out, and then I tried to shovel what was on the floor back in with my hand.

"What the fuck is that?"

I glanced up at him, vision blurred with tears. "It's my grandmother's ashes."

"What? Holy shit…" He squatted down beside me and tried to help.

158

Smacking his hand, I snapped. "Leave it alone! Just leave me alone!" I finished collecting what I could and I stood up, hands shaking, clutching the box to my stomach.

Everyone in the room was staring at us. At me. With horror. Disgust. Though there was sympathy from Sapphire.

Appalled, I started walking, faster and faster. By the time I got to the hallway past the kitchen, I started running. Tears were choking me, and for a second I thought I was going to throw up.

In my room, I slammed the door shut behind me and locked it.

I sank to the floor.

chapter eleven

*B*ACK AGAINST THE DOOR, *I* gave in to my emotion and cried for the first time since my grandmother had died.

Mortified that his friends had seen that, devastated that he hadn't been honest with me, I hoped like hell Devin would deem his duties as host more important than me.

I jumped when a hard knock shook the door. "Tiffany, let me in."

But I had choices for the first time in my life and I chose to ignore him.

Devin wasn't a man capable of being ignored though. "Goddammit. Let me in."

I stayed silent.

"This is my house," he said. "Open the fucking door."

Of course he would pull that shit. He was the boss when it was convenient for him. My alleged friend otherwise. It didn't work that way. I was one or the other. An equal, or not.

"Go away, Devin. Please." My voice trembled.

But he used the lock pop to unlock the door and he pushed. My face went into my knees and I gave up, scooting out of the way so he could come in. I didn't want to fight. I was hurting too much. My chest felt like an elephant was sitting on it, and I hated myself for being so stupid as to fall in love with a man that was more than inaccessible to me. He was in orbit as far as I was concerned. I could never reach him.

He slid in and closed the door again. Then he sat down next to me, knees up, arms resting on them. "I'm very sorry about your grandmother," he said, voice sincere but careful.

"Thank you." I was still clutching the box. "We weren't close."

"I know. But I also know this had to have been really hard for you. Why didn't you tell me?"

"I don't know." But as I hugged the box and my knees, I knew that wasn't true. "Maybe I didn't want you to offer to come help me. Maybe I didn't want you to see where I grew up. Or see how people treat me." Like I was less of a person than they were. He seemed to hold me in some sort of esteem, or so I'd thought. I didn't want him to see that I wasn't worthy of him.

"I would never judge anyone for poverty. I'm not like that. I know I've been fortunate. Lucky. If anything, I would have appreciated seeing it because I know your childhood created you. And you're strong, with a solid moral compass, and some of the most admirable qualities I've seen in any human being."

I didn't feel strong. I felt like cotton, wispy and soft, easily blown around by the wind.

Devin turned to me, and with his thumb he reached out and

wiped a tear off my cheek. "You amaze me," he said. "Every day I watch you, astonished that you're so strong, so true, so honest, and every day I fall a little bit more in love with you."

My heart squeezed and I had a monstrous lump in my throat. Never had I imagined he would say that his feelings for me were so strong as to call them love. I had hoped, wanted desperately for him to care, but love? It seemed too fantastical to be true. I forced myself to ask the question. "Why didn't you tell me you're not actually divorced?"

"It wasn't a secret. I just didn't really give much thought to it."

"I find that kind of hard to believe."

We were almost touching, but not quite. He shrugged. "I told you about Kadence, that she's difficult. But maybe I still didn't want you to hear about the shitty details. It's a terrible ending to a marriage and I know you'd never find yourself in a situation like this."

His logic didn't seem sound, but then, maybe mine didn't to him either. We had a choice- we could choose to be angry with each other or we could move on, and I had never done anger well. It had the power to destroy. So I let it go. "You couldn't have predicted that she was going to be so miserable about a divorce." She had cheated on him after all.

"I knew she would do this. She's used to getting her way." He gave a sigh of exasperation. "I made you sit there tonight because I wanted to force you to see the world I live in. I wanted to make you see that I'm not worthy of you, because sometimes you look at me like I'm this perfect man, and seriously, Tiff, I don't deserve that."

"It's a persona, Devin. I see the real you."

"You do, don't you?" His voice was gruff. "I didn't think you were ever coming back and that scared the shit out of me. I thought you'd disappeared, that I had fucked it all up by being an asshole when you told me you're a virgin." He reached over and pulled one of my hands down, lacing his fingers through mine. "I actually thought maybe you'd made up your grandmother being in the hospital to get away from me, but then I realized immediately that wasn't something you'd do. You'd never even think of it. But how fucking sad is it that it even occurred to me as a possibility? That's what marriage to Kadence did to me."

"She sent those pictures." It wasn't a question. It was obvious. I should have pressed earlier, but I hadn't wanted to annoy him by prying.

"Yeah. I want you to know I never cheated on her. I didn't date until we were legally separated and we would be divorced already if she had been even remotely reasonable about it. I didn't take my marriage vows casually."

I believed him, but I wasn't sure what that meant. What any of it meant. "What now?" I asked, because I needed to know what he was thinking, what he wanted. I needed to know if I could find the courage to walk back into the family room the next morning and face all his famous friends.

He didn't reach for me beyond our clasped hands. I wished he would. I craved his reassurance, his touch. His love.

There was no hug, embrace.

Instead, he shocked me with his next words.

"I'm going to sell this house. I never wanted it. And with it liquidated I can throw some money at Kadence to speed up the divorce."

live for *me*

I barely heard the latter part of what he was saying. "You're selling the house? I guess you won't need a housesitter then," I said, shocked. He wouldn't need me. I wouldn't have a job or a place to live.

Or the ability to see him every day, bare chested, coffee mug in his hand, smiling a good morning to me. I wouldn't get to walk along the coast with him, Amelia running ahead of us. Or have him patiently teach me how to take a left turn in his car. I wouldn't have him.

"No. I won't need a housesitter. Maybe you can go to school," he said, like it didn't particularly matter to him one way or the other. "Become a nurse like you planned."

"Where am I supposed to live?" I asked, afraid to look at him, afraid he'd see my raw emotion, my vulnerability, my hurt. He didn't want me to live with him any more. I was too young. Too virginal. It hurt deep inside, like a deep lacerated wound, pulsing, aching with each heartbeat, blood pumping out in a hot, agonizing gush. It was worse than any slap because the pain wasn't going to subside. Not a brief sting that would fade. It was going to keep going on and on, each day that I was gone from him.

"Well, where do you want to live? You can go to college anywhere you want, right? Haven't you always wanted to see Florida?"

But I shook my head, violently. "No. That's too far away." I couldn't imagine being that far from Maine and everyone I loved. From him.

"Too far from what?" He was stroking my hand now softly, slowly.

164

"From home. From you." I sounded miserable. I felt miserable. I didn't even care if my words sounded pathetic or juvenile. The thought of being hundreds of miles away from Devin, never seeing him ever again, tormented me.

"Good. Because I don't really love Florida. I would have bought a condo there if you wanted me to, but it's not my first choice."

I swiveled to look at him. "What are you talking about?"

"I'm not going to let you go to Florida without me." He gave me a sly smile. "What would be the point in that?"

"Don't tease me," I said in warning, even as hope sprang up eager and obnoxious. "It's cruel."

Devin leaned over and kissed me. "I'm not teasing you. Not now. Not about this. Tiffany, all I want is to be with you, because I love you. Do you realize that?" His gaze burned into mine. "I *love* you. In a way that is so huge and overwhelming, I am not even exactly sure what to do with it."

I stared at him in wonderment. Devin loved me. He felt it, too, that overwhelming and all-consuming love that had been growing and growing between us. It was the kind of emotion that never left me. It went everywhere I was, infiltrated every thought, sat in my chest like a helium balloon.

My throat felt tight. "I love you too."

He gripped my hand harder, his expression intense, searching. "I'm really glad to hear that. Say it again."

With a sigh, I cupped his cheek, slid my hand back into his hair. "I love you," I said, the tremor gone from my voice. I spoke with confidence, and deep, boundless emotion. There was no need to pretend it was only friendship or hide from my feelings.

live for *me*

"I have never been happier than I have been here, with you."

"I came here to run away," he murmured. "It was meant to be both an escape and a punishment and instead I found you."

Setting the box down carefully, I shifted closer to him. "I came here to be alone. But I'm so glad I'm not."

"I've lived selfishly, but you make me better." He took my face between his hands. "You're so sweet, do you know that? I look at you and I think how is it that you found your way here, to me, in the middle of nowhere Maine, when I live in a city with eight million people. I had no idea that first night that you would burrow into my heart and make a home there." He smiled. "Like a chipmunk. That's what you are."

I laughed softly. "Wow. Thanks."

"Chipmunks are adorable and so are you."

I couldn't be annoyed with the comparison. I knew I wasn't traditionally beautiful, but that he saw anything adorable in me thrilled me. I could see he meant it. He looked besotted, a mirror to my own image.

"First an owl, then a chipmunk."

"I'm not very romantic, am I?" he said, his voice gruff, his forehead resting on mine. "This is different from what I've felt before. All I know is that you're here." He thumped his heart. "And I think that if you were to leave me a piece of it would be torn out and I would bleed to death."

"That sounds pretty romantic to me," I whispered. "Thank you."

"God, don't thank me. That makes it seem like I'm doing something for you, a favor, when the truth is, it's the opposite." Devin rubbed his lips over my temple and I closed my eyes briefly.

He felt so good, so masculine, so loving. So mine. It seemed unreal, like this couldn't be happening. But it was. His touch was possessive, his kiss tender.

"I look at you and you're content, grateful for your life, and I think I don't have any right to be an asshole about anything." The next kiss he gave me was deep and passionate. "God, I love you."

"I love you too." Our lips met again and again and I poured my heart into each one, wanting him to feel and read and understand that he had me for as long as he wanted me. "I can't believe this is happening."

"It's happening. This has been happening since the minute not that I laid eyes on you, but the minute you spoke. You captured me with your words."

"And suddenly now I can't think of anything to say."

"Just kiss me then."

So I did.

He guided me down onto the floor and his hand worked its way under my shirt, our kisses getting more frantic, urgent. My legs wrapped around his ankles and I realized I was lifting my hips to meet his, desire overcoming reason.

Emotion and arousal were taking me to a place of no return, our touches more greedy and desperate than seductive.

I pushed at his shoulders before we went any further. "Devin," I breathed. "We have to stop. All your friends are in the other room."

"So? They won't hear anything." He bent down to kiss me again in the dark.

"But they'll know. I can't go back out there… after."

"We don't have to go back out there until the morning then."

"Then they'll really know!"

"Are you embarrassed for them to know we're together?" he asked, eyebrows drawing together.

"No, of course not. I mean, I'm sure they're going to be really surprised, but if you're okay going public, I'm fine with it." I was. It might actually make it tolerable to be in their company if they knew that I wasn't just Devin's weird little housesitter who had no purpose in being at their party. "I just meant I don't want them to know we're having sex right now."

"We are?" He waggled his eyebrows. "I must be doing it wrong then."

Laughing softly, I smacked his arm. "I'm serious."

"But if they weren't here, you'd have sex with me?" he asked carefully.

I nodded, swallowing hard. I was just a teeny bit terrified, but I loved him and trusted him.

"Holy shit, okay. I thought we were just making out. I can kick them out." He was already halfway to standing up.

"What? No!" I sat up, laughing breathlessly. "You can't do that. We'll just have to wait until they leave in two days. In two days, right? Or are you really going to celebrate New Year's Eve on a jet crossing each time zone?"

"Not unless you want to." He held his hand out to help me on to my feet. "I'd prefer to spend it alone with you."

I rose. "I'd like that." I suddenly felt shy, eyes darting to the floor. I didn't know how to be Devin's girlfriend. Was that what I was? I wasn't even sure.

He touched my chin and tilted my head up. "Hey," he said softly. "Marry me."

The world actually tilted. I swore for a second everything, sound, time, came to a screeching halt and tipped the World As I Knew It. "What?" I whispered. "Are you serious?"

"I wouldn't have said it if I wasn't serious." He tucked my hair behind my ear. "We already know we can live together without conflict. I don't want this to be casual. I want to know that you're committed to me. To us."

I had already committed my heart to him. There were so few people I was truly drawn to, that I opened myself up to. I had shared my genuine emotions with Devin, allowed him to see my fears and insecurities. I was committed to him. To us. Without question, with or without marriage. That he wanted me the same way I wanted him astonished and humbled me.

My choices were limited. His were boundless.

Yet he was choosing me. Of all the women he could be with, he wanted me.

"Is that really what you want?" I asked, quietly, giving him an opportunity to change his mind. "People will talk, you know. They'll say things about our age difference, give you a hard time. They'll say you're slumming." And worse.

He nodded. "It is very much what I want. I want to call you my wife. You have more maturity than women twice your age, and people will talk no matter what, so whatever. I can handle the gossip."

Then I wasn't going to worry about it. I had been the subject of gossip my whole life. People had trashed my mother. Trashed my father. Trashed me. Let the gossip bloggers call me ugly and a gold digger. It wasn't anything I hadn't heard before and what did I care? I knew who and what I was. I put my arms around him.

"Yes."

"Yes, what?"

"Yes. I will marry you," I said simply. "After your divorce, of course."

He laughed softly and kissed my temple, his lips brushing over my skin. "I'll double the lawyer's fee to get him moving. You've made me very happy. And just so you know, I'm sneaking into your room later after everyone else is asleep."

I laughed, an expression of the pure joy I felt. "You are not."

"Uh, yes, I am. I'm not going to be denied the feeling of sleeping with you in my arms for the first time."

A shiver of excited anticipation ran up my spine. The idea of being able to slide up next to Devin in bed and rest my head on his chest, without any questions or awkwardness, sounded like perfection. "If you insist," I said.

"I do. Now are you coming back out there?"

I nodded. "Kiss me, Devin. One more time."

He bent his head, amber eyes darkening. "I love hearing my name on your lips. My real name."

"Devin," I whispered.

"Tiffany," he murmured. "My heart belongs to you."

I DIDN'T EXPECT OUR ABSENCE TO go unremarked on, and it didn't. As soon as we reappeared, Lizzie stopped sucking on an olive suggestively and stared at Devin's hand on the small of my back. She said, "Oh, my God, what was that all about? Were you seriously carrying a dead person's ashes in that grocery bag? WTF."

"Lizzie," Devin reprimanded. "Show a little fucking

sympathy."

But this was only the beginning. I knew that. The sign of things to come. Everyone was going to have something nasty to say to me once they realized that the plain loser girl from Maine had scored Devin. But I was so high on his love that I didn't even care. Let them hate.

"Have you ever lost someone you care about?" I asked Lizzie, slipping onto a stool at the island where she leaning. "A parent or grandparent? A friend who died?"

For a second she looked caught off guard, but then she turned mulish. "Of course. Everyone has."

"So you get that it's a little hard to let go after only five days."

"Whatever."

Jay, who had never spoken to me, shook his head. "Lizzie, sometimes you're just a bitch, you know that?"

"Fuck you," was her response to that. "So what's the deal with you two?" she asked then, gesturing between Devin and me. "G, is this seriously your new little fuck buddy? Pedo alert."

"You're the one dressed like a twelve year old hooker," he told her. "And you need to either keep your opinions to yourself or take yourself back to the city because I'm not going to listen to you insult Tiffany."

"Rawr," she said, making mocking clawing motions. "Sorry. I didn't realize you were so attached to your new toy."

"Liz, come on," her boyfriend said, taking her hand and tugging her away from the island. "Let's go upstairs."

"Why?"

"To keep you out of trouble." He gave her a smile and smacked her backside. "And to get a little action. Come on, baby."

live for *me*

I wasn't sure if he was doing it out of kindness or if he really did just want to have sex, but he managed to lure her away and up the stairs, Lizzie laughing as they went. With her gone, the tension in the room disappeared. No one else asked any questions, and I sat there, sipping a soft drink and listening to their conversation about business, fighting the urge to grin. I heard the chatting in the kitchen, but I was mostly focused on my own thoughts, on Devin's words in my room. He loved me. That was all that mattered.

Sapphire sat down next to me and gave me a smile. "Don't worry about Lizzie," she told me. "She just hates when she's not the center of attention. It's a common personality trait in this industry. Most of us are attention whores."

I smiled back, grateful that she was making an effort to talk to me. "It's okay. I understand that everyone is wondering why a nobody is at their party."

"Girl, don't downplay yourself like that. Everyone is somebody." She studied me. "But be careful, okay? Men like G, they're used to getting what they want. Doesn't mean they're not good men. But no one tells them no."

While the warning was clearly well meant, I didn't want to hear it. Not right then. Not when I just wanted to wrap Devin's words around me like a warm blanket and hold them to me. "I don't plan to tell him no," I said, quite simply.

Her eyebrows shot up. "Well, all right then. I guess you know what you're about."

"I do." I reached over and touched her arm, wanting her to understand that I really did appreciate her warning. "Thanks. You're being really nice to me. I appreciate it."

"You seem different," she said. "I like what I see. I just don't want to see that destroyed." Her long pointy fingernails smoothed her platinum hair down the side of her head. "But G is a good man."

Devin heard her last comment as he came up behind me and kissed the back of my head. "Thanks, sugar," he told her. "So did Tiffany tell you we're getting married?"

Her hand dropped to the marble countertop. "Excuse me? No, she did not tell me that."

His arms had wrapped around me from behind and I felt enveloped, supported, even as I tried not to let Sapphire's response make me uncomfortable. Of course she was going to react with surprise. It was shocking news.

"Yep. She was smart enough to say yes to me and now she's committed. I'm not letting her go ever."

I was grinning. I couldn't help it. He sounded so enthusiastic, so happy. His embrace was strong, warm. I leaned back against his chest.

"Well. Congratulations," she said, raising her cocktail glass. "All the best."

"What are we toasting?" Ray said, wandering over with a bottle of scotch in his hand.

"G and Tiffany are engaged," Sapphire told him.

"You shittin' me?" He sounded a little drunk, which was confirmed when he moved to clap Devin on the shoulder and stumbled a little in the process. "Congrats, bro."

"Thanks. I couldn't have picked a better girl." Devin finally let me go and reached for the glass he had abandoned earlier.

"Hell, you could have picked anyone and she'd be better than

live for *me*

Kadence," Jay said. "That bitch is crazy."

It wasn't exactly a ringing endorsement for me, but I'd take it.

The other woman, Cassandra, had wandered over and while she happily accepted another cocktail, she didn't look like she cared one way or the other what Devin's plans with me were. Given the glassy eyes, the cocaine and the alcohol were mixed with a third substance. My guess was heroin, based on a former foster sibling, but I didn't know for sure. I did know I was glad when after another twenty minutes she and her husband disappeared.

"Let's go, boo," Jay said to Sapphire. He gave a fake yawn, followed by a wink. "I'm tired. March your sexy ass up those stairs."

She rolled her eyes, but she did stand up. "Goodnight, G." Then she startled me by leaning over and giving me a hug. "Goodnight, Tiffany."

"Goodnight." I hugged her back, pleased. I knew she wasn't that much older than me, at the most twenty-five, but she seemed so much more experienced, wise. It made me feel good that she was willing to accept my relationship with Devin.

We were left alone in the kitchen, Devin kissing the side of my neck. "Well, I guess this means I don't have to sneak into your room after all."

"Shouldn't we clean up?" I asked, glancing around at all the sticky surfaces, the half-eaten appetizers, the dirty wine flutes and martini glasses.

"Are you insane? No." Devin nuzzled further down, tugging at the neck of my sweatshirt. "The housekeeper can do it."

"I am the housekeeper."

174

"Not anymore. Now you're my girlfriend."

I shivered. I hadn't thought about what that meant. Not exactly. I didn't want to either. That was for later. Right now, I wanted to retreat into my room with Devin, away from harsh lights and potentially prying eyes. I slipped out of the bar stool with the intention of going with him to my room but it had the effect of taking me out of his reach. He frowned.

"If you start cleaning up this kitchen I swear I will throw you over my shoulder and drag you kicking and screaming out of here."

I raised an eyebrow. "That's a bit ridiculous and dramatic. I was just standing up."

"Oh. Good." He smiled. Grinned, actually. "Let's go to your room."

"That's what I was planning to do. And for the record, if you ever try to throw me over your shoulder and take me anywhere, I will pack and leave." I knew he was teasing, but at the same time, he needed to remember who I was. That nonsense wasn't going to fly with me. I'd been at the mercy of other people my entire life. I had no fantasies about being dominated by a man.

He didn't get angry.

Instead he laced his fingers through mine and raised our hands so he could kiss my knuckles. "I'll never make you do anything you don't want to do. You have my word on that."

His reassurance meant the world to me. "Good. Because I definitely don't want to move to Florida."

"No one is moving to Florida." He kissed me, the kind of loving, sensual kiss that made me sigh.

"Are you really selling this house?"

"Yes. Let's start fresh with a house that doesn't have bad memories."

"But all my memories here are good." I didn't want to leave Richfield. I'd been happy there. I'd met him, had gained my freedom. We'd created a home together, complete with a Christmas tree and our dog. Because I had absolutely emotionally adopted Amelia, and she had me as well.

"Then we'll keep it." He kissed my earlobe, tugging it gently between his teeth. "Whatever you want, love. Anything you want is yours."

"All I want is you," I whispered.

chapter
twelve

WE WENT INTO MY ROOM, Devin carefully closing the door behind us and locking it. Amelia had padded in quietly along with us, and she went and lay down on the blanket in the corner I had put there for her weeks earlier. The room was dark and I stood there, unsure what to do. Devin moved around the bed to the bathroom and flicked the light on, flooding the room with a bright beam.

It made me shield my eyes, but immediately he pulled the bathroom door closed, leaving it only open a few inches, just enough to keep us out of total darkness.

I stood there, awkwardly, hands stuck down into my pockets, rolling on my ankles. But then I remembered the box I'd left sitting on the floor and I bent over and picked it up before it accidentally was disturbed again. I wasn't sure what I was going to do with my grandmother's ashes, but I had the idea that I might walk down to the beach come spring and toss them into the ocean. I couldn't imagine I'd want to keep them forever, but I wasn't ready to get rid of them right away either. So I carefully pulled open the top drawer of my dresser and slid the box in there.

"I'm really sorry," Devin said. "About your grandmother, about knocking the bag out of your hand."

"I know." I shut the drawer. "It's okay."

"If there is anything I can do to help with anything, let me know."

I nodded. "I appreciate that. We can talk about it later. I'm not really ready to deal with it, but it means a lot that you're here for me." It was a novel feeling and I was both basking in the idea and balking from it. I didn't know how to graciously accept help. It hadn't been offered to me very often, and sometimes even when it was, it had strings attached.

When I turned back, he smiled, his arm outstretched. I took the hand he was offering. He led me to the bed, and my heart was racing, with nerves and anticipation. I didn't want to disappoint him again. I knew that I had before Christmas. Not that he would ever say that, but I knew.

Urging me onto the bed, he kissed me before pausing to yank his shirt off. I reached up and touched his chest, endlessly fascinated by those muscles he had there. He didn't have any tattoos on his chest, and I was glad. I didn't want the distraction. I just wanted his smooth skin and the hard, masculine, underlying motion. Devin bent over me, his belt buckle hitting the button on my jeans, his arms holding him up so he didn't crush me. His hair fell forward and I reached up, sliding my fingers into the silken strands.

When his mouth covered mine, I opened my lips automatically, wanting that intimate sweep of his tongue over mine. He didn't just comply, he made love to my mouth with his touch, leaving me breathless, body restless, burning. He didn't touch me anywhere, just kissed me endlessly, like he couldn't possibly get enough of the taste of me. I shifted my hands so that they were on his back, gripping him, pulling him closer to me.

Finally when my lips were swollen and my breathing was ragged, he sat back on his knees. Tugging at my sweater, he said, "Sit up. Let's take this off."

I half sat up and let him pull the shirt over my head. But he made no move to take my bra off too. My necklace thumped back against my chest. It was a tiny heart on a cheap chain.

"What is this?" he asked. "I've never seen you wear this."

"It's always under my shirt." It was so small it was likely he hadn't even noticed it when we'd gotten partially undressed in the family room after putting up the Christmas tree.

"Where did you get it?" He fingered it, the tiny heart dwarfed by his long fingers.

"It was a Christmas present the year I turned ten. From my foster mother. She was diabetic and she wasn't mobile, so I did a lot of housework there, but she was very kind to me." When Devin dropped the necklace, I rolled it between my fingers. "She told me that I had the two greatest gifts a girl could hope for-intelligence and a good heart."

"She was right." He rubbed his thumb over my lip. "Both of yours are immense. What happened to her?"

"She died."

"Jesus." Devin shifted so that he was lying beside me. He

live for me

pulled me against him, snugly. "You amaze me."

"Why?" I wished he hadn't asked about the necklace. Or that I hadn't answered. It had shifted the mood from seductive to solemn.

But Barb had been a very special woman and I couldn't relegate her gift to a conversation to have later. She was one of those stops along the way that had given me strength and courage and hope. Somewhere I imagined she knew that, or I hoped she did.

"Because you've survived some really shitty situations." His fingers traced lazily back and forth across my stomach. "We don't have to do this all tonight, you know. We can get there one step at a time."

He was talking about sex. "Please don't treat me like I'm fragile. I'm not."

"That's not what I meant. But you're inexperienced."

"So were you, once. And how did you get experience?" I asked. "By doing."

He kissed me, pulling my bottom lip into his mouth before releasing. His amber eyes were dark in the muted light. "Are you sure you want to do this?"

"Are you sure *you* want to do this? Because I'm starting to wonder." A girl couldn't help but get a complex when a guy was hesitating that much.

"Of course. I want you so bad it's killing me," he murmured. "But I'm afraid of hurting you. Of taking it too far."

"I trust you." I did. "And this time I promise not to blurt out any awkward confessions right in the middle."

"Never be afraid to share your feelings." His fingers had

shifted lower, over the front of my jeans, to stroke between my thighs. "You can tell me anything."

God, that felt good, but it was barely anything. Such an unfulfilling tease. "Then I'm telling you that I want you. Now."

His fingers were just dancing around my thighs, lightly scraping over my labia, my clit, down even lower. It caused goose bumps to pop up all over my flesh, and an ache stirred to life. "Fine," he said, his tone teasing. "Jesus. Bossy."

I stuck my tongue out at him.

While he popped the button on my jeans, he buried his head in my neck and flicked his tongue over my skin. "Brat."

"If I'm a brat, I think that makes you an asshole," I murmured back.

He laughed softly, taking my zipper down. "I never claimed otherwise. We're both walking around with our arms folded across our chests, aren't we? I guess that's why we understand each other."

"Yes. We do." I sucked in a breath when he moved his hand inside my panties. I hadn't been anticipating that and his long, warm fingers stroking through my moist heat had me letting out a soft moan.

"You like that?" His tongue dipped into my bellybutton as his finger sank inside me.

I nodded, even though I knew he couldn't see me. But he glanced back up at me, removing his hand immediately.

"Oh," I said in disappointment.

"Take your clothes off," he said. "Stand up and undress for me. Prove to me this is what you really want."

I immediately hesitated. "I'm not a stripper."

live for *me*

"I'm not asking for a dance routine to go with it." He sat up. "Here, I'll show you what I want." Devin rose off the bed and stood next to it, facing me.

I rolled on my side to better see what he was doing, palms sweating with nervousness. There was no way I could just stand in front of him and strip. I couldn't expose myself like that. But it didn't mean that I didn't want to be with him, that I didn't want him to take my virginity. I did. And I knew he would give me pleasure. I just wanted it to be in the dark, with him covering me with his own body. I didn't know how to be overtly sexy.

He took his zipper down and shed his jeans, kicking them off his feet. Then he peeled his boxer briefs off and ended up standing in front of me completely naked. His thighs were muscular, his stomach the same, fit and with intriguing lines I wanted to explore with my tongue. I swallowed hard, a hot rush of desire flooding both my mouth and my panties. He was hard and sexy and he was mine.

More than my lover. More than my boyfriend. My future *husband.*

The man I loved. I would be his wife and that was more amazing than any of this.

His erection bounced a little as he moved closer to me and I stared at it. It was fascinating, all smooth skin, tight testicles capping the bottom of his shaft. Without thinking, I reached out and touched it, curious what it would feel like. When he groaned, I looked up at him in question. "What?"

He didn't answer the question. He just said, "Stroke it. Please."

I wasn't sure how to exactly, but I experimented, gripping him, and sliding my hand up and down the length of him. I could tell when he approved, because he made a sound in the back of his throat and his erection actually jumped a little in my hand. But there was too much friction to comfortably stroke him any faster so I tentatively covered the tip with my mouth, knowing salvia would be helpful. I may not have been a sexual expert, but it wasn't like I didn't have a clue what was what. I had watched movies, even what could be considered porn, out of curiosity. I'd seen blow jobs, or emulations of them. I never went into any situation without doing my research. But watching was easier than doing.

Devin murmured my name. "That's right, baby, I like that a lot."

It was all the encouragement I needed. I tried to take him all the way, but I didn't open my throat and didn't get very far. But I did manage to succeed in lubing him up with my saliva, so I went back to stroking him with my hand, this time much more successfully. I tested squeezing him tighter, and was rewarded with a soft curse. I explored his balls, tickling over them, amazed at their tight skin.

But Devin put his hands on my head and tilted me so I was forced to look up at him. "If you're doing this to get out of taking your clothes off, you can just stop. I'm not changing my mind on that."

"No," I said, shocked. "I did it because I wanted to touch it. You." I still didn't think I could stand in front of him and bare it all, but my body was responding already to his, to the sensation of his skin, his scent. To his clear arousal.

"Good. But just so you know I'm not taking your clothes off. So if you want them off you have to do it. Standing up. I need to know you're not going here, doing this, just to please me."

"Don't you trust me?" I asked, even as my nipples tightened at his words. He sounded like he wanted to thrown me down and fuck me hard, but he was restraining himself completely. I wasn't sure how we'd gotten there, but I did know that I was one hundred percent turned on and ready to have sex with him. "I won't manipulate you. That's not me."

"You're right. I'm sorry. Of course that's not you." He bent over and kissed me, hard. "I need to go find a condom."

"I have some."

"You do?" Devin looked scandalized.

Climbing off the bed, I went to my bathroom. "It seemed good to be prepared." For him. I had bought them on a trip to town, on impulse. Impulse and optimism.

"I don't even know what to think about that."

Quickly retrieving them, I went back to the bedroom. Devin was sprawled out on the bed, gloriously naked, hands behind his head. The sight brought me up short. He was hot. I wasn't sure I was truly entitled to all that sexy man.

But I knew that I had been brought to Richfield for a reason. That I was entitled to him, and his love. That maybe he was my reward for a lifetime of loneliness.

"Don't think anything about it all. Just use it." I tossed the condoms down next to him on the nightstand.

Then I took a deep breath and stood next to the bed. I knew him well enough to know he wouldn't back down, and if he wasn't feeling indulgent, he wasn't going to give in. For whatever reason, he wanted me to be the one to take my clothes off. I didn't want to at all, but I had to. I had to prove to him that I was adult enough to satisfy him, that I was a woman. That I wasn't willing to have sex with him purely for his pleasure. I wanted the pleasure for me as well.

So I started to take down my jeans, wiggling to get them off. Devin just watched me, slowly, carefully. When they were at my feet, I bent over and pulled them off. This wasn't so hard. I didn't feel uncomfortable. I peeled my socks off too, then reached behind me for my bra hook. But then I realized that would be a better thing to do standing up, not bending over. Getting a little flustered, I shot back up, elbows at an odd angle, hands still behind my back.

Without any urgency, Devin reached over to the nightstand and pulled the box of condoms towards him.

"What are you doing?" I asked.

"I'm hard. I want you desperately. I'm putting a condom on to help me control myself."

"Do you really want me?" I asked, hating myself for asking it. But doing it anyway.

"God, yes. I want you the way I've never wanted anyone ever."

That was enough to have me popping my bra hook and sliding the straps down my arms. I held the cups against my breasts in a last attempt at modesty. At hiding myself from him. But then I realized Devin had already seen all there was to see of me. He'd seen inside me. He'd listened to my thoughts, my heart. It made total sense that he should be the one man I could trust to see my body completely bare.

So I dropped the bra.

Took down my panties.

And stood in front of him, heart racing, mouth hot, but

confident.

"You're beautiful," he said. "I am the luckiest man alive."

Somehow, when he said it, I believed him.

When he held out his hand for me, I took it, climbing on top of him. I didn't know what I was doing exactly I just knew I wanted to feel my skin on his. I laid my chest on his, legs over his, the soft hair on his thighs tickling my flesh. We both sighed. It felt delicious. Intimate. Everything I had always imagined.

He lowered my head to his and there was nothing between us, no barrier, physical or emotional. I didn't kiss him immediately. I just touched his face, slid my foot over his calf, drew my lips across his earlobe, inhaling his scent. When I did kiss him, it was slow, languid, our understanding of each other complete, our needs in tandem.

But when my hips starting to roll against him, questing, as I felt his erection pressing into my thigh, he suddenly flipped me onto my back.

"What?" I asked in question.

"I don't have the condom on yet," he said, taking my nipple into his mouth and suckling it. "Too dangerous in that position."

"Oh." I hadn't even thought about that. When he moved between my thighs, I spread my legs instinctively. For a second I tensed, anticipating him entering me, but he just continued to lick and suck my breast and nipple, while I heard the rustling of the condom wrapper.

"Relax," he murmured, taking his tongue down my stomach, teasing it into my belly button. "We're not there yet."

In a way, I just wanted to get it over with. To kill the fear, the suspense that maybe it would hurt, maybe I would hate it, maybe he would be disappointed.

But I slowly forgot to think about it as he explored my body with his hands, his mouth, his hair tickling my chest, his fingers teasing inside me briefly before disappearing again. He seemed to be in no hurry, and had no particular plan in mind. He just stroked and sucked and kissed and touched until my nails were digging into his shoulders and I panted from need. My head fell to the side as he sucked on my swollen clit, a soft groan escaping my mouth.

He pulled me apart, blew on me, then worked me with his tongue until the heels of my feet were digging into the bed and my hips were bucking.

That's when he stopped.

Right before I could orgasm. The sudden shift had me crying out in dismay.

But then I realized why. He moved up, between my legs, his erection nudging against me. He used one hand to hold himself up, the other to keep me wet. He pushed inside, just a little and I squirmed on the bed, partly from the odd sensation and discomfort, partly from the physical need for more. For completion. He gave a few strokes, in, out, just the tip of his cock in me, his eyes locked on mine.

Then he pulled out completely and I was surprised that I missed the odd fullness, that small invasion.

"Devin..." I didn't understand what he was doing. He was back at me with his tongue, massaging my folds with his fingers, tongue pushing deep inside me. "Oh, my God." I bit my bottom lip as pleasure sent shivers all over my body.

When my hips started to rock onto him and my moans grew

louder, Devin again abandoned me.

I squeezed his arm in total frustration. He kept taking me right to the edge.

But this time when he pressed against me, I welcomed it. I wanted that pressure, that hot push of his cock. He went slightly deeper this time, stroking in and out while his finger teased me apart, allowing me to accommodate him further. I thought he was going to take me then, all the way, but he didn't. He pulled out completely and this time, I tried to keep him there, feeling frantic. I wanted him deep inside me.

My hips followed him, but he still pulled out entirely. "That's not fair," I told him, grabbing his rock solid ass and trying to move him back into place. He was way stronger than me though and didn't even budge.

His eyes were dark, hair falling over them. "What isn't fair, love?" His voice was gruff.

I shook my head. I didn't know how to articulate my feelings. I wasn't even sure what was happening, exactly. I just knew that I couldn't hold any thoughts in my head and my thighs were trembling and my voice was hoarse from moaning. So he went back to what had clearly been his original plan. He dropped his mouth down onto my clit for the third time, his beard tickling along my vagina. All my nerve endings seemed to have been amplified and I felt like I might shatter into a thousand pieces if he didn't do something soon.

Needing an orgasm, I tried to quiet my moans, tried to stop my hips from rocking so he wouldn't recognize how close I was and I could come before he could pull away. But Devin knew what he was doing and just when I thought I would be allowed to explode, he removed his mouth and gave me a sly smile. "Nice try."

This time when he moved between my legs, I welcomed him. I lifted my hips for him, I wrapped my legs around his ankles. I gripped his ass and encouraged him to move closer to me. He didn't start out as he had before, teasing and slow. This time, he just plunged into me and I caught my breath in shock at the sudden fullness of penetration. But it wasn't painful. It was what I had been wanting, waiting for, and as he stroked in and out, his breath hot and frantic, my inner muscles contracted and I exploded in a tight, intense orgasm.

I clung to him, shocked, unable to breathe or make a single sound as ecstasy washed over me. He looked as shocked as I felt.

"Holy shit," was his opinion, his thrusts increasing in speed, his eyes drifting briefly shut.

The room was starting to spin behind him and I realized I was clenching my vagina onto his cock in an instinctive response to the pleasure.

"Breathe, Tiff," he told me in a harsh command.

I hadn't even really realized I wasn't and I let out a huge whoosh of air and dragged another back in, my body falling slack against the mattress. "Devin…"

He gave a tight groan and his rhythm changed, his eyes clamping shut. When they reopened a minute later, I asked, "Did you?"

I didn't know what a man's orgasm felt like. It seemed like he had, but I wasn't sure.

"Fuck yes," he said.

He rested his forehead on mine for a second and I felt his

hot skin, heard his ragged breathing. Inside me, there were aftershocks, though he didn't feel as big. Devin kissed me then pulled back and collapsed on the bed beside me. "Are you okay?" he asked. "Did it hurt?"

I nodded, suddenly feeling like I was going to cry. It felt like something hugely monumental had just happened to me. This was real. We were real.

"Is that yes, you're okay, or yes, it hurt? Or yes to both?"

"I'm okay. It didn't really hurt." There was a throbbing now, an awareness of my vagina I wasn't used to, but it wasn't a bad feeling. My body felt satisfied, still tingly. "I came," I added, though I realized immediately he knew that.

He studied me, searchingly, up on his elbow. "I'm really glad you did. Kiss me."

I did but it was a quick kiss. I felt too overwhelmed. Tears were silently rolling down my cheeks.

Devin wiped them. "Hey," he said softly. "You can tell if it hurt or if you didn't like it. You be honest with me, remember?"

"And you lie to me?" I sniffed. I wasn't sure why I was crying. I just knew that everything had changed, that I had allowed that wall in front of my heart to come crashing down. It felt amazing and wonderful to be with Devin, but so powerful it was like I couldn't contain it inside me. It burst forth in unexplainable tears and words that sounded distrustful.

"No. Of course not." He stroked my hair. "I was just saying that you can tell me anything. Don't sugarcoat it if you didn't enjoy it. I want to give you pleasure. Make you happy."

"You do." I wrapped my leg over his, wanting him closer to me. "I've just never been in love before."

"Neither have I," he said hoarsely.

That he meant it was something I didn't doubt. I studied the outline of his lips, ran my fingertips down his arm. "I feel… wrapped in it. Does that make sense?"

"Perfect sense." He lay back down and pulled my hip over so we were snug up against each other.

I'd never slept naked before but I didn't want to cover back up. I wanted the moment to last indefinitely. Devin pulled the condom off and tossed it on a tissue on the nightstand. He tucked the comforter over me.

"Is Amelia okay?" I asked, glancing over at the dog.

"Are you kidding? She's snoring."

When I paused to listen, I realized he was right. She was softly snuffling in the corner. "She needs a dog bed in here too."

He kissed my forehead. "Order one online for her if you want, beautiful. Or we can get one next time we're in town."

It all seemed so normal then. Like everything would be the way Devin and I had already been living, only now knowing that he loved me. If I had been happy before, then I would living in perfection now.

Our house, our dog, our love. Our lives.

Perfect. Together.

I drifted off to sleep in Devin's arms, never anticipating it would be the only time.

chapter
thirteen

A HARD KNOCK ON THE DOOR had me jerking awake. For a second, I was confused why there was a heavy weight on my stomach, but I realized it was Devin's hand resting there. My heart was racing from being jerked out of sleep and I turned my head towards him, checking to see if he was awake. Maybe I had dreamed there was a knocking.

He breathed deeply through his nose, his eyes fluttering open. "What the hell was that?" he mumbled.

The knock came again, confirming it was real. "Someone's at the door," I said, stating the obvious. "I can't answer it. I'm naked."

"What do you want?" Devin called loudly. Shifting a little he kissed my shoulder.

Feeling exposed, I pulled the comforter up tighter over me, even though there was no way anyone could just walk in. Devin had locked the door. Scrambling for my phone, I squinted to see what time it was. Six am. This wasn't exactly the romantic morning after I would have hoped for, but I did like the feel of Devin's body alongside mine.

"It's Lizzie."

Wonderful. I looked at Devin in question.

He just shrugged and gave a pronounced sigh. "What do you need?"

"Cass OD'd. Sam just called for an ambulance."

"Shit." Devin sat up quickly. "Are they on their way?" he called back to her. "Is she still breathing?"

"Yes and yes." Lizzie's voice had lost the attitude of the night before. She sounded tired, sad.

I sat up myself, horrified. I should have mentioned to Devin that Cassandra had seemed off. She'd been beyond drunk. Devin was already pulling on pants without any underwear. "What hospital would they take her to?" he asked me.

"Good Samaritan is the only one in town," I said, scrambling out of bed.

He waited until I reached the bathroom and slipped inside then I heard him open the bedroom door and head out into the hallway, his voice muffled as he spoke to Lizzie.

I winced at the bright light and hurried up with my business, aware of how tender I was down south. Washing my hands, I paused briefly to look at myself in the mirror. I didn't look any different. Funny that even though it was ridiculous that I would, I still expected some sort of visible change to my features. Or an older and wiser expression. A member of the club.

But no. I still looked like me. For the most part, I felt like me.

Hurrying, I went back in the bedroom and got dressed. When I made my way to the kitchen, I saw Devin pulling on his T-shirt and stuffing his feet into his shoes. "I'm going to the hospital. Do you mind staying here with everyone else?"

I shook my head. "No, I don't mind." I didn't want to go back to that hospital anyway. It was where my grandmother had just died and I didn't think I could face those hallways, the nursing staff.

Lizzie was hugging herself, wearing nothing but a tight T-shirt that said Fuck Off and a pair of pink panties. Sapphire and Jay were sitting on the couch, talking quietly, Sapphire in a big fluffy robe, Jay's arm around her. Lizzie's boyfriend wasn't around. "Where's your boyfriend?" I asked her.

"Sleeping."

Nice.

Devin put his coat off and came over to me and squeezed my hand. "I'll call or text as soon as I know anything." Then he turned to the others. "No social media. No one say a goddamn word to anyone until we can do damage control. I have a call in to PR already."

There were half-hearted nods.

That would have never occurred to me. Damage control. As if ingesting enough drugs to overdose wasn't damaging enough, there were careers, livelihoods at stake. Their minds were always on the spin, and that was a world I didn't understand. Though I figured everyone did the same thing, just on a smaller level. Most people didn't want to advertise their addictions and problems.

But it still made me sad. All of it made me sad. Cassandra was beautiful and talented. Successful, wealthy. Why did she need to seek escape? I wasn't judging her, I just felt bad for her.

Devin left through the garage and I stood there, not sure what to say or do. Suddenly Lizzie made gagging sounds and ran to the kitchen sink and threw up, hair falling into her face. I went up next to her and pulled her hair back off her face, rubbing her back. "It's okay," I murmured. "Cassandra will be fine."

Lizzie stood back up, but she clung to the sink rim, eyes watery. With the back of her wrist she wiped her mouth. "I'm fucking hungover. And I feel guilty as fuck. I brought that heroin. It was from Kadence when I saw her a few weeks back and I don't use. But I knew Cass does and it was meant to be a New Year's gift to her." She looked at me and gave a harsh laugh. "I gave her a gift that could have killed her. What the fuck is wrong with me?"

I wasn't sure what to say to that. I just tore a paper towel off the roll and got it wet. Sapphire had come in and she folded her arms over her chest.

"Look, it's not your fault, Lizzie. Sure, you brought that shit, but Cass would have gotten it from somewhere else if you didn't. This whole casual drug use is bullshit though. No one can control it. No one is invincible."

I handed the towel to Lizzie, who wiped her mouth and hands. "This is going to be all over the Internet in about five seconds. Devin can't control it. Someone at the hospital will talk."

"And her album downloads will go up." Sapphire shook her head. "It's a fucked up world we live in."

Not feeling like I had anything to contribute to the conversation I started cleaning up the kitchen. There were bottles and plates and glasses everywhere. Lizzie stared at me while I did it. I don't think she realized she was, but she just leaned on the counter and watched me, her nipples stretching the cotton of her T-shirt. Sapphire started helping me, grabbing some plates and bringing them to the dishwasher.

"You don't have to do that," I told her. "I've got it."

"I didn't grow up rich. I can load a damn dishwasher," she said.

Her platinum hair fell forward in a sleek curtain as she did just that, her crazy long nails clicking against the racks as she filled them.

"Thanks."

"No problem."

Lizzie didn't make any motion to join us. She looked like she was in shock. "Does anyone want any coffee?" I asked.

"God, I'd love some," Sapphire said.

Lizzie nodded, biting her fingernail. Then without warning she said, "Did you think the heroin was bad? Like that black heroin or whatever?"

Sapphire shrugged. "I don't know. It's possible. Anytime you inject shit into you it's possible it's bad."

I had finished a sweep of the kitchen collecting trash and after washing my hands I started the coffee machine, patting my phone in my pocket, reassuring myself it was there. No word from Devin but he was probably just arriving at the hospital.

"I was just thinking maybe Kadence was trying to kill G. Or cause a scandal by having someone die at his house."

Pausing the middle of scooping out coffee grounds from the bag, I waited to hear Sapphire's opinion. No one was that crazy. Were they?

It was a stupid question. Of course they were. I had

encountered crazy, cruel, selfish, plenty of times in my life.

"Who the hell knows?" Sapphire said. "But that seems like a dumbass way to get your man back."

It made me uncomfortable to hear them talking about his estranged wife. I fervently wished he were actually divorced but I suddenly felt like I had done something wrong. I had slept with a married man. So he was trying to not be married. He was still married. You didn't just get to decide you weren't anymore. Only the court did that. It seemed like a justification that he was emotionally done and everything I'd been feeling, all those warm and happy thoughts, seemed dulled by the reality of Kadence. And Cassandra.

So much for bliss.

"G might get back with her. You never know."

"Girl, you have no fucking tact," Sapphire said in exasperation. "Do you not see Tiffany standing right here making your skinny ass coffee? She does not want to hear your opinions on G and Kadence."

Well, she had that right. I definitely did not. Though at the same time, even though it was awkward, I was curious what Devin's friends thought about Kadence and his relationship with her. If these were his friends. It was hard to really say if there were genuine friendships or if they were just clients.

"Oh. Sorry," was Lizzie's apology. She looked at me, still chewing her nail. "How did you meet G?"

"I'm the caretaker here," I said, taking the carafe and filling it with water. I wasn't going to let Lizzie's rudeness bother me. It wasn't even the worst that was likely to come my way in the future. I figured I should be prepared. "Housesitter. Whatever you want to call me."

"And you're fucking him? I mean, not that I blame you, I totally would too, but you know he's just out of his marriage. He's going to want to date around."

My cheeks warmed. I didn't want to sound naïve or defensive so I just poured the water and said carefully, "Devin and I have talked about our relationship." What we had said was none of her business. I believed truly and deeply that he loved me. She wasn't going to ruin how special that felt.

"What are you, a lawyer?"

Jay came in to the kitchen. "Who's a lawyer? And do I smell coffee?"

My phone vibrated in my pocket. I pulled it out and let them continue talking, grateful Jay had interrupted Lizzie. I had a feeling she was just getting started on interrogating me and I had no interest in going there with her.

It was a text from Devin.

Cass doing ok. Going to transfer her to rehab tomorrow. Sending a car to take everyone to airport. Need to be ready by 3.

"Is that G?" Sapphire asked.

I nodded. "He says Cassandra is okay and they are transferring her to a rehab facility tomorrow. He's sending a car at 3pm today to take all of you to the airport."

"Party's over," Jay said, shaking his head. "I wonder if that jet for tomorrow night ever got scheduled."

There was a second text from Devin.

Your jeep is showing up today. Keep a lookout for delivery guy. Xoxo

I liked the added hugs and kisses. They made me feel better

about the whole weird situation. Last night was starting to feel like a dream. Like it wasn't real.

Pouring myself some coffee, I said, "I'm going to take a shower. Does anyone need anything before I go?"

They all shook their heads, Jay already reaching for his own coffee mug.

Back in my room, I saw the used condom on the nightstand and I gingerly picked it up and carried it to the bathroom, lip curled. When I went to get clean clothes and panties from my dresser, I also spotted a blood smear across the pristine white sheets. Apparently I had bled and didn't realize it. I tore the sheet off and bundled it up. Something about that stain seemed harsh. Why was it the reality of sex wasn't as romantic in the daylight then it was at night?

But I knew it wasn't that. It was the uncomfortable feeling that I was alone. That instead of feeling Devin's arms wrapped around me or having him tease me as he tossed out the condom, I was doing it alone. There was no leisurely breakfast together, no morning sex. I felt selfish and immature for even thinking about myself when Cassandra was in the hospital, but I couldn't seem to stop myself.

When I came back out, clean and feeling better, Lizzie was also dressed in leather leggings and an oversized sweater hanging off one shoulder. There was a knit cap on her head. She was drinking a glass of white wine. "Some dude just dropped off a jeep. He said G ordered it. Jay signed for it."

"Oh, okay, thanks." I was kind of glad I didn't have to deal with the delivery man. It felt so overblown to have a jeep delivered to coastal Maine.

"Is it for you?" she asked slyly.

"Yes."

"I knew it. But it was kind of obvious when the license plate says TIFFANY." She gave me a grin. "I guess being a housesitter isn't a bad gig."

"It's a Christmas gift," I said. "Devin is very generous."

"You could call it that."

She wasn't going to make me feel cheap about his present. I went to go look at it out the front window. There it was. A Tiffany blue jeep sitting in the driveway, looking very shiny and new. Lizzie was right. The Maine license plate stated TIFFANY on it. That was a little embarrassing. A lot embarrassing. So not me.

"It's a sweet ride," Lizzie said.

Damn it. Couldn't she just leave me alone for five minutes? "It's very nice."

"Don't you ever get excited about anything?" She sounded annoyed. "It's a fucking car!"

Her annoyance annoyed me. "What am I supposed to do? A cartwheel? Devin's not even here to see it. And that's not my personality anyway."

"What personality?" She stomped off in a huff.

I had no idea why anything I said or did mattered in the slightest to her, but it hurt my feelings. I had a personality. I'd just learned to rein myself in. It caused nothing but trouble to call attention to yourself in the foster system. I couldn't wait until Lizzie left to go back to New York. I was going to welcome the quiet again after this ridiculous house party.

I texted Devin.

The jeep is beautiful. Thank you. Xoxo

As soon as the guests were gone, I was going to go out in the driveway and sit it in. Smell it's newness. Touch the seats, the dashboard. Marvel that it was mine. But I didn't want Lizzie rubbernecking at me while I did it.

Glad you like it. As soon as we get back from NYC we can go get your license.

Wait a minute.

Back from NYC? I thought I was staying here.

What? No, of course not. You're going with everyone at 3. The car will take you from the airport to my apt and I'll meet you there tomorrow.

I didn't now whether to be terrified or excited. I was going to New York City. Just like that.

How long?

Couple days.

What the hell was I supposed to pack? Anxiety gripped me. I called Cat. She answered on the third ring.

"He is taking me to New York. I'm going to puke."

"What? OMG. That's amazing. I mean, unless you don't want to go to New York."

"I do, but I don't know what to pack. I don't have a city wardrobe. I have a thrift shop wardrobe."

"Lucky for you, that's in style now." She added, "So… everything went okay when you got back, obviously."

I wanted to tell her details, but I was in the front hallway by the main stairs and anyone could walk by at any given moment. I didn't want to share any of my news where it could possibly be overheard. "Yes, it definitely did. I'll call you tonight and tell you everything. But I just had to tell you because I'm freaking out."

live for *me*

"Well, shit, have fun! Don't freak out. Just enjoy it!"

"You're right. Thanks." It wasn't a vacation since Devin was making arrangements for Cassandra and probably had work to do, but it was still exciting. I was leaving Maine. For the first time ever.

After I hung up I sent another text to Devin. It was important to remember none of this would be happening if Cassandra hadn't overdosed. I hoped she was totally recovered.

Is Cass ok?

Yeah. She was lucky this time.

I'm glad to hear it.

Me too. I miss you.

That made my heart swell. I missed him too. A whole hell of a lot. I didn't know how to navigate with his friends. I felt like the poor girl from the backwoods that I was.

Miss you 2. Should I send you a selfie? :)

Funny. Love you, owl.

*F*LYING WAS AWFUL. IT WOULD have been scary enough with someone I was comfortable with, but being with a group of strangers who were rich and jaded, it was horrible. I felt like I couldn't tell them I was worried, and I felt stupid every step of the way when I didn't know or understand the process.

"What are you doing?" Lizzie snapped at me at one point when I hesitated getting on the plane.

She had run into the back of me when I stopped walking.

It was a miracle they were even letting me board the plane since all I had was my birth certificate and my high school ID

202

card with my picture on it. But it was a private jet, so I guess the rules were different. It was so small though, I panicked when it was time to duck and go inside.

"Go ahead," I said, stepping to the side on the steps.

"OMG." She huffed past me, curls flouncing.

Sapphire raised her eyebrows at me. "You ever been on a plane before?"

I shook my head, swallowing hard. "But I'm fine." It was like walking into a new foster home. I just needed to straighten my spine and do it.

So I did. But that didn't mean I enjoyed any of the hour long flight. Takeoff was unnatural and terrifying. Looking out the window made me want to hyperventilate. Lizzie and her boyfriend, whose name I still didn't know, bickered the whole time. Sapphire and Jay slept. I had taken my laptop and I tried to work on my story, but I was distracted by every sound and motion the plane made, sure we were going to drop out of the sky and crash into a field.

When we finally landed I relaxed my shoulders for the first time since takeoff. I stood back and watched and followed behind everyone else as we got off the plane, collected luggage and found the man with the sign that read GOLD. There were a lot of people. Possibly more people than I'd ever encountered in one place at the same time. I clutched my purse, backpack on my shoulders, and felt very small, insignificant. Lizzie had already questioned my lack of luggage, but all I had was my duffel bag and my backpack, so I had opted for the backpack as less conspicuous. Devin had said only a few days, so how much did I really need?

But between Lizzie, Sapphire, and the retrieved luggage from Cassandra's room, there were eight enormous bags going with us. Designer. I read enough gossip blogs to recognize how expensive the luggage was.

It was then I realized, as we were walking through the airport, that Lizzie and Sapphire were attracting huge amounts of attention. They were both wearing high heels, full makeup, and big sunglasses. Dozens of people were gawking, pointing, snapping pics with their phones. And there were paparazzi. I recognized them by the giant cameras they held, flashes going off as Sapphire turned and gave them a wave, flashing both her nails and her bling.

Jay and No Name Boyfriend strolled behind, Jay in his cashmere coat, looking every inch the millionaire that he was.

In contrast, I felt like people must think I was a ballsy fan who had attached myself to them.

Or that they had adopted me a la the Jolie-Pitts, given that I looked about fourteen years old next to all their glam.

"I love you, Lizzie!" some twenty-year-old guy yelled out.

She blew him a kiss.

It all felt ridiculous.

The car waiting for us was a limo. I stared at it in astonishment.

"Don't let it freak you out," Sapphire said, give me a nudge with her elbow and a smile. "It's just the easiest way to get us all there. Plus the windows are tinted."

"Don't you ever get tired of people staring at you?" I asked her. I was being totally sincere. I wouldn't enjoy it. Not that I wouldn't enjoy people appreciating my talent, because I would. If I could sell a short story or novel, I'd be all over that shit. But

I didn't want people following my every move and snapping photos of me every time I stepped out of the house.

"Not really. I guess I'm used to it." She slipped into the limo and I followed her. "Besides, I don't wear this wig for Jay."

Lizzie sank into the seat across from us. As soon as the door shut behind the guys she took off her glasses and rubbed her temples. "Holy fuck, I have a headache. I need a drink."

"Maybe you need to eat something," her boyfriend said. "You always get bitchy when you're hungry."

"Fuck you, Alex," she said.

Alex? I never would have guessed his name was Alex. He looked like a Joaquin or something with his exotic looks. Alex must have been his real name.

"I rest my case," was his opinion.

We pulled out of the airport terminal and I strained to see everything around me as we exited. But all I could see was other guys, and apartment buildings jammed alongside the highway. I had never seen buildings that close together or so close to traffic. It was claustrophobic. The car motion was also making me sick, with its gunning of the engine, then slamming of the brakes. The man driving never looked back, never spoke to any of us. There was a man in the passenger seat who appeared to be some kind of security guard given that he'd met us at the plane and escorted us the whole way.

I breathed through my nose carefully and leaned against the window.

After we went through a tunnel we emerged in the middle of buildings. They were just everywhere, all around us. I looked out the window and tried to crane my neck to see the sky but I couldn't get the proper angle. I knew I looked like a hick staring wide-eyed at everything but I couldn't help it. I'd seen all of this on TV but never imagined it would feel so… condensed. Even from a car. I did notice though that the diversity of people walking was just as it was portrayed on TV. There was every size, shape, color of human being possible, with eclectic fashion choices.

My phone buzzed.

You in the city?

Yes. It's crazy busy. Lol.

The doorman knows you're coming and will let you in.

Ok. Thanks.

We dropped Lizzie and Alex off first, pulling up to a high rise with tiny balconies that jutted out towards the river. Then after another nauseating twenty minutes in stop and start traffic, we dropped off Sapphire and Jay. She squeezed my hand and gave me her phone number before she got out. "Call me if you need anything. For real. You don't have to feel stupid about asking any questions or if you're just bored or whatever."

"Thank you." I squeezed her hand back. "I really appreciate that." I did. But I wasn't going to call her. It might be intimidating, but I was going to do this on my own. I was going to stay at Devin's apartment by myself and then in the morning, if all went well, I was going to see my father. I'd been researching online using his name and age and I was pretty sure I had found the right guy. After an exhaustive online stalking of him, I had determined he worked at an office in mid-town Manhattan. I just wanted to see him. Just once. From a distance. Just to see if I would feel anything.

Maybe if he looked nice I would take the plunge and contact

him online and see if he was receptive to meeting in person. At the very least, I wanted to let him know that I wasn't dead, despite what my grandmother had told him.

I hadn't thought that I would be able to see him this soon, but if I was here, on my own, it was something I wanted to jump on.

At the same time, though, I found I was desperately missing Devin. I wanted him with me, sharing my first taste of New York.

After Sapphire and Jay went into their building, we finally got to Devin's apartment, or at least I assumed we were. I wasn't really sure. The driver turned back to me when I didn't make any move to get out of the car.

"You're here, miss."

"Okay. Thanks." I grabbed my backpack off the seat then jumped when the security guy opened the door for me. "Oh, thanks." When I got out on the sidewalk I stared up in shock. The building was a glass sculpture squashed in between brownstones. It was a modern design and the whole thing seemed to be tilting forward towards the street in a way that was both cool and terrifying. It was clearly a trendy neighborhood too, given the people I saw walking around and the numerous street-side cafes.

I went to the door and was about to open it when it opened for me. A man in a uniform smiled at me. "You must be Tiffany. Mr. Gold said to expect you. I'll take you up."

I smiled back. "Thanks."

He chatted the whole way up in the elevator and I tried to give appropriate responses but the truth was, I was exhausted and overwhelmed. I smiled and nodded and told him my flight was fine when he asked. But I wasn't great company. He forged ahead though, telling me the amenities the building had to offer and when the maid cleaned and how I could ask the concierge for anything, including ordering food or having drycleaning sent out. The thought of sending out clothes to be washed made me want to laugh.

"Oh, and Mrs. Gold is in the apartment but she said she'll be leaving in about twenty minutes. She's just packing some clothes."

Was he fucking kidding me? Kadence was in the apartment? There was no way Devin could know that. I was about to protest, maybe ask the doorman to direct me to a coffeeshop so I could call Devin but we were already there and he was already throwing open the door for me.

chapter fourteen

"**M**RS. GOLD," THE DOORMAN CALLED. "Mr. Gold's guest is here."

"Thank you," a woman's voice responded from somewhere in the apartment.

Then suddenly there she was. Devin's wife. She looked older in person than she did in photos but at the same time she actually looked less artificial. She smiled and held out her hand to me, catching me off guard.

"Hi, I'm Kadence. I'm sorry for still being here. I had hoped to be gone before you got here, but I didn't realize I still had so many sweaters in the apartment." She gave a laugh. "I suppose I could just buy new ones, but I happen to like some of them, you know? Sweaters are like woobies. They're comforting."

In fact, she was wearing a sweater with black skinny jeans and high heel boots. "Come on in and I promise to be out of your way in a flash."

"Thanks," I said, because what the hell else was I supposed to say? "I'm Tiffany." I shook her offered hand. "Mr. Gold's housesitter."

By all accounts, she was crazy, so I didn't want to piss her off. Just let her leave and I could lock the door and take a nap.

"Housesitter?" She winked at me. "Okay, that's what we'll call it." Then she waved to the bellman. "Thanks, Joshua. I'm going to miss you."

"You, too, Mrs. Gold. Stop by and say hi sometimes." He gave us both a smile and a wave then left, closing the door behind him.

I waited for Kadence to start snarling the minute the door shut and our audience was gone, but she didn't. "Devin told me you're seeing each other," she said breezily, walking back down the hallway. "I would say you're a definite improvement over that bitch Brooke. Devin brags about how intelligent you are."

This was all news to me. Like WTF. Devin spoke casually to Kadence about me? She approved? This was not the way any of their relationship had been presented to me. It had to be a con. She had to be disarming me so that she could go in for the kill. "Thanks," I said in response, suspicious but not wanting to let her know I was. "I've never met Brooke but the word online is she has amazing abs."

Kadence laughed. "That's about all she's got going for her. My maltipoo has more brains than her." She stepped into the kitchen, which was sleek and modern, the total opposite of Richfield. "Wine?"

"Sure." The hell with it. I needed something to get me through this nonsense. I dropped my backpack on the floor and leaned against the counter. "So what went down at Prada?" I asked, totally curious. If I had to be there with Kadence I might as well hear what she had to say.

"Oh, my God, that bitch bag knew I was going to be there. I had an appointment and Devin mentioned it in casual conversation, apparently. So then we're all there- like awkward- because he totally forgot I would be there at that time and then she starts in on that whining shit." Kadence took a sip of her wine then cleared her throat. "Daddy," she said, in perfect imitation of Brooke's voice. "Buy me something!"

I laughed. I couldn't help it. "I've heard that particular voice from her in the background on the phone. So obnoxious."

"Right?" Kadence shook her head. "God, I don't understand how anyone can spend five minutes with her without wanting to punch her in the vagina. But that doesn't seem to matter to men. Boobs over brains, every time."

Considering she herself was sporting a pair of DDs, which were most likely not natural, I thought that was a bit ironic. "Then I guess I'm screwed," I said, oddly amused.

Glancing around the apartment, I wasn't sure who had decorated it. I wasn't even sure what Devin's actual taste was. This apartment was very modern, with sleek furniture and very little color. It was mostly wood tones, glass, chrome. The only color came from vases and throw pillows in neutral greens and browns. It was smaller than I would have expected, but this wasn't Maine. I realized I had gotten used to the space at Richfield. That was even more ironic than Kadence's cup size.

"Well, Devin seems happy with you so keep yourself natural."

She handed me a glass of white wine. "If I had to do it over, I think I would skip the boob job and get a master's degree. Men who respect your mind don't care when it ages."

Was she implying Devin left her because of her age? He'd said she'd lied to him when they first met, said she was younger. I took the wine. "I would look ridiculous with a big chest. It is what it is."

"You have the kind of face that will still look fresh at fifty. Just remember to wear sunscreen."

"Will do. So who picked out this apartment?" I asked, curious. I should have felt uncomfortable with her, but I really didn't. I didn't feel threatened in any way. Though I supposed in thinking about the pictures with the angry words on them I should watch her around the knife drawer.

"Devin picked the apartment. He wanted to be in the East Village because of the vibe. But I decorated it. He has really shitty taste. If you gave him free rein everything would be neon. He bought me a yellow car. It was so gross, but I still have it because I didn't want to hurt his feelings. He means well. He is a generous guy, despite his general grumpiness."

Nothing about what she said seemed untrue, exactly. I hesitated but then I asked what was probably a very loaded question. "So why aren't you divorced yet?" But then I heard how rude it sounded and I took a sip of the wine. "I'm sorry, I guess that's none of my business."

Her eyes narrowed but she didn't go ape shit on me. "Because dividing assets is always complicated. Look, if you've been reading stories online about me being crazy, just ignore them. I swear to God, a woman can't be upset about her marriage ending without everyone deeming her crazy. I didn't want a divorce. I was sad, grieving. I wanted to fight to make it work. I don't think that's all that unexpected after six years together."

It all sounded so reasonable. So believable. Was she really that good of a liar?

"I don't begrudge Devin his happiness. I just wish it could have been with me." She shrugged and waved her hand. "But God, why are we talking about this? It's almost a new year. Here's to new beginnings."

"I'll drink to that." I was in a completely different place than I had been twelve months before. My life was totally turned upside down, and while the night before I thought I had it all figured out and was ecstatic, now I was completely confused.

What was truth and what was fiction?

I remembered Devin telling me if I were honest with him, he would lie to me. It was a joke, a tease. But now it suddenly seemed like I didn't know the man I had agreed to marry.

Who was still married.

To a woman who seemed anything but crazy.

"Do you have any heroin?" I asked her, after draining half my glass of wine.

She started and looked at me like I was insane. "Excuse me? Uh, no. And I'll be honest with you, if you're a smack addict I feel like I need to warn Devin. Dating a junkie is an emotional roller coaster, not to mention expensive."

Okay, now I was really unsure what was what and who was who. "No, no, I don't do drugs either. Someone just told me that you have them."

Kadence frowned. "You know, people need to just shut their

fucking mouths for a change. I swear, are we all still in middle school?"

I had to agree with her there. "It seems to be a hobby for some people."

"I've got better shit to do than talk about people. Don't you?"

"Uh, yes." I had my opinions but I'd never really been in any position to trash talk anyone else.

"Okay, so I just made fun of Brooke. But that was different. I think your ex-husband's twit of a girlfriend is open season."

The wine was already going to my head. I hadn't slept enough the night before because I was well, losing my virginity to this woman's still-husband. Who in between her and me had dated a twit. The anxiety of Cassandra's overdose, dealing with Lizzie, getting on a plane for the first time, and finding myself in Manhattan and out of Maine for the first time had me physically and emotionally drained. I had eaten very little on top of all that, so after only one glass, I had a pretty strong buzz going.

"I'm pretty sure that Brooke is talking about you, so I think you're well within your rights."

"What until she hears about you." Kadence raised her eyebrows. "Are you ready to deal with haters?"

"I've been dealing with haters my whole life." I smiled because I was getting drunk faster than I would have thought possible. "Fuck 'em."

She laughed. "A toast. To our haters." She raised her glass. "Fuck 'em."

"My glass is empty."

"Well, shit." She refilled it.

Which is how I wound up drunk with my fiancé's wife.

Kadence left an hour later but by then I was basically wasted. I lay down on the couch, face down, still clothed, shoes on, no blanket over me.

She had taken a rolling suitcase full of sweaters.

I had taken to heart the message that not everything was quite as black and white as I had thought.

Before she left, she showed me the doll of herself. The very same doll I had seen at Richfield. It danced in front of my eyes, the whole room spinning behind the blond hair, the plastic smile. For a second I thought I was going to throw up but I swallowed my bile and kept it all in.

"Isn't this so creepy?" she asked. "But Michael had it designed for me as a Christmas gift three years ago and I couldn't tell him I thought it was hideous."

"That was nice of him," I said, yawning, my head resting on the arm of the couch. It didn't make any sense to me that the doll was at the apartment. I could have sworn I saw it at Richfield just a couple of weeks before. On Devin's bed. Then in his garage.

"I wonder why Devin keeps this thing." She shrugged. "Oh, well. I'm taking it with me. It is *me* after all. I don't imagine you want it here."

"No," I said honestly. "Not really." But then I felt guilty that I didn't want her doll so I amended, "It's a very beautiful doll. I just don't think I'm a doll person."

"I don't think you are either." She made the arm of the doll wave at me. "Bye. Maybe we can do lunch sometime if you're going to be in the city for awhile. It's been really nice to hang out with you."

"It's been nice to meet you, too." Kadence was surprisingly a hell of a lot easier to be around than Lizzie.

Then I passed out.

WHEN I WOKE UP, I had drool on my face and a raging headache. "Oh, my God," I moaned to the empty apartment. I had to pee so bad I thought I was going to wet my pants, but sitting up and walking seemed impossible. I didn't even know where the bathroom was. I gagged when I raised my head. So I gave up and just lay there, swallowing repeatedly.

When the need to throw up passed, I carefully slid my phone out of my pocket with trembling fingers. There was a text from Devin twenty minutes earlier saying he was on his way to the apartment. Fabulous. It was eleven already. I'd been sleeping for twelve plus hours. Or passed out, however you wanted to label it.

The door to the apartment opened. "Tiffany, baby? I'm home."

"Hey," I said weakly, when he came down the hallway, his bag over his shoulder. Amelia ran over to me and licked my face.

I turned my head to escape her slobbering kiss, though I did stretch my hand out and attempt to pet her.

"Tiff? What's the matter?" Devin came over to me and felt my forehead like I might have a fever.

"I'm hungover," I admitted. My voice sounded hoarse and foreign to my ears.

"Hungover from what?" He sounded shocked.

"Wine. Kadence and I shared two bottles."

He had been bent over me and now he stood straight up again, raking his hair back out of his face. "Excuse me? You got drunk with my wife?"

Funny how suddenly she was his wife, not his ex-wife. When had that happened? "I thought she was your ex-wife."

"You know what I mean. Why were you with Kadence?"

"She was here, in the apartment, when I got here. She was packing up sweaters."

"So you just got drunk together?" He sounded horrified.

"She was playing hostess. I didn't know what else to do but talk to her. I didn't have any right to kick her out. She clearly had a key or whatever and she did have clothes still here." And why did I have to defend myself? That seriously annoyed me.

I managed to sit up, though the room spun and bile crawled up my throat.

"Oh, my God. This is just classic Kadence. So what bullshit did she tell you about me?"

"Actually, all she said about you was that you have bad taste in home decorating."

His eyebrows shot up. "What? I do not. And seriously? That can't be all she said."

"She said that she never wanted your marriage to end and that she wanted to fight for it, but you had already checked out and started seeing Brooke. She said Brooke is an idiot, which I agreed with. But also that you and she had discussed me and you seem fond of me and my intelligence."

"Not right now," he muttered.

Ouch. That stung. I wanted to reprimand him, but I didn't have the energy.

"Why didn't you just call me? I would have come back sooner."

Briefly closing my eyes, I said, "By the time you would have gotten here, she would have been gone already."

"I could have called her."

"And told her what? To get the hell out? What would be the point in that? You'd just antagonize her. It was no big deal, in the end. Which is what's so weird about it." I rested my head in the palm of my hands. "Holy shit, my face feels like it's going to explode."

Devin went into the kitchen. He pulled out a glass and filled it with water. He came back and handed it to me. "Here. I'll go downstairs and get you some aspirin from the desk."

"Thanks." I sipped greedily. My mouth was thick and dry, with a sour taste. The water was too cold though and it hit my stomach hard. I gagged and coughed. "This is awful. I've never been hungover. I don't like it."

He shook his head. "Unbelievable. She's a fucking piece of work. Next time, if she's here and you don't want to argue with her, just turn around and leave. Go downstairs and call me. But I'm going to change the locks and have a word with the doorman."

"He seemed fond of her."

"Because she blew him on a regular basis. I found that out a couple of months back."

I frowned. That sounded so crude. I had a hard time reconciling all the things he'd said about Kadence with the woman I'd met the night before. I also didn't like how sometimes it felt like Devin was telling me what to do. I knew he had more life experience but it just felt like he was in charge and I was... his employee. Even though I wasn't anymore. I didn't think.

"Where's the bathroom?" I asked, forcing myself to stand, though I was hunched over a bit.

"You haven't been to the bathroom yet?" He shook his head. "I guess this was a bad idea. I should have left you at Richfield."

Because that was what I wanted to hear. Not. "Why? Because I've never been to New York and I didn't know the etiquette for tossing sort of ex-wives out of my boyfriend's expensive apartment? I flew on a plane yesterday for the first time in my life with people who don't even like me. I was worried about Cassandra, worried about you, I didn't eat all day. I was tired, stressed, and totally unprepared for Kadence so all in all I think I did okay."

He looked immediately contrite. "I'm sorry. I'm not upset with you."

"Gee, thanks."

Devin made a face. He touched the ends of my hair and gave me a smile. "I'm looking forward to showing you the city. It will be fun. And I'm not your boyfriend. I'm your fiancé, remember?"

"When are you going to be divorced, Devin?" That was bothering me. Really, truly weighing on me.

"As soon as Kadence is reasonable. God, I just can't stand her and her manipulations. It's like she enjoys tormenting me."

I nodded, but I didn't like what I was hearing. He was angry. Kadence had sounded anything but. I didn't know the full story. I imagined no one really did but the two of them. It bothered me that I wasn't sure he was telling me the whole truth. It also bothered me that I could spend months, years, potentially living with him as his mistress. That's what it was. If he was married, that's what I was.

Devin showed me the bathroom and I shuffled inside, shutting the door behind me. I pulled down my jeans with trembling fingers and sank onto the toilet with a sigh. Wine was clearly not my friend. I didn't even understand why people drank it if this was the after effect. I peed for about twelve minutes straight, my bladder clearly over capacity. I looked around the room. More modern design. Dark wood and shiny white tile. It was tidy, with nothing resting on any of the surfaces. No tissue box. No scented candle. No magazine rack.

The only sign that this wasn't a hotel was the wastebasket, which had a box stuffed into it. A white box with a pink strip across it.

That was a pregnancy test. I'd seen the brand enough times in the tampon aisle. It had been opened. Finishing up my business, I washed my hands, then took some toilet paper and pulled the box out of the wastebasket. Inside the foil had been opened and the test stick was just rattling around. Tentatively with the toilet paper I pulled it back out. The test was positive.

Oh. My. God. I turned and finally lost the battle against my stomach, throwing up into the toilet. I flushed quickly so Devin wouldn't hear, but he was already knocking on the door.

"You okay? I'm coming in." I hadn't locked the door and he opened it and swore when he saw me half bent over the toilet. "You need to eat something or it's going to linger all day."

But I just wiped my mouth on my sleeve and stood back up. "Who is pregnant?" I asked.

"Huh?" He gave me a blank look. "I have no idea."

I picked up the stick with the positive line on it and shook it at him. "This was in the trash! Who the hell is pregnant?"

"I have no idea." He glanced down at the stick in horror. "That was in here?"

"Yes. So either this belongs to Kadence or there are other women who are free to come into your apartment when you're not here that I don't know about."

"No one comes in here. This is my apartment, not a hotel."

"Then Kadence is pregnant." I tossed it back down on the counter. It clattered across the shiny marble surface and fell into the sink.

"Then I guess we should send her a gift." He stared at it, a smile tugging at the corner of his mouth. "If she's knocked up, then clearly she has a new guy she's trying to trap. That means she'll be more agreeable to the divorce."

"Are you sure it isn't yours?" That was my real fear. That if it wasn't Devin's she wouldn't have taken the test there. She would have done it in her own apartment.

"Yes. I'm sure," he said coldly. But then a flicker of doubt crossed his face.

"When was the last time you had sex with her?"

"Right before I came to Richfield. We had a mediation appointment. It got intense, emotional."

He didn't look away or express any shame or remorse. He just stared me down, defiant.

That had only been a couple of months. When I had met him, he was fresh off a nostalgia fuck with Kadence. "Then you don't know if it's yours or not." I tossed the pregnancy test back in the trash and washed my hands. I splashed water on my face.

"I guess not. But most likely not. That was months ago. She would have told me already. She'd be showing."

"That was only ten weeks ago." I dried my face with the hand towel. I suddenly felt calm, removed. I couldn't do this. I couldn't be this person. Swept up in drama and lies, his world of drugs and money and manipulation.

I came to Richfield with nothing but my dignity, my intelligence, and my moral code. I couldn't stay there with less. I couldn't trade any of that for love. It felt wonderful to have Devin hold me, to look in his eyes and know that he did love me. That I was special.

But I couldn't live with myself if I accepted the arrangement the way it was. I would ultimately be ashamed of myself, and I would feel insecure. I would be dependent on him, clingy. He would run the show and I would be the stage crew. Yes, I loved him. I loved him more than anyone else I'd ever met, with a love so deep it hurt at the same time it healed, yet as it was, I couldn't be his equal.

It felt like a game I didn't know how to play, with angry express packages, lawyers, over-the-top gifts. "I need to go home," I told him.

His eyebrows shot up. "Back to Richfield? Not today. We can go back tomorrow. Don't you want to see the city?"

"No, I mean to Vinalhaven. I'm not going back to Richfield and I'm not staying here with you."

"What do you mean, exactly?" His voice lowered, his eyes narrowed. I could see the anger brewing.

"Devin." I reached up and touched his chin, running my thumb over his unshaven skin. "I love you. But I can't do this. It's not me. I can't live with you while you have a wife and maybe a baby and friends who overdose in our family room."

He grabbed my hand and held it to him tightly. "I love you, too. Doesn't that count for anything?"

"It does. It really does." Tears filled my eyes. "But I feel like I'm losing myself. Or maybe I never knew myself. I'm nineteen instead of eighteen and I've never seen or done anything. I want to live on my terms for the first time in my life, not compromise."

"You can do anything you want with me," he insisted. "Don't do this. I won't have house parties. I'll talk to Kadence, we'll make sure she doesn't come in the apartment."

"And if this is your baby?"

"Then I'll take care of it. I'm not a total asshole. I try to do the right thing, which is why I've never played dirty with Kadence. I could have, you know."

"I'm sure you could have. I think you're a good man, I really do, and that is why I love you." Tears ran down my cheeks. "If you'd like, call me when the divorce is final."

He kissed my hand. "You're not leaving me. I'm not going to let you. You're the best thing that's ever happened to me."

It was the hardest thing I'd ever done, but I stepped away and moved around him. I couldn't do it. I couldn't stay and lose myself. I might enjoy it now, but I would wake up in two years, five years, and hate myself.

Devin grabbed at my arm but I walked faster, tears coming harder. I checked my pocket for my phone and as I moved across the apartment, I grabbed my backpack off the floor and slung it over my arm, swiping my coat off the kitchen counter.

"Tiffany, what are you doing? You're not going to just leave." Devin sounded unconvinced that I was really doing just that.

"I have to," I pleaded. "I can't hide at Richfield and pretend that nothing else exists. That's what we've been doing."

"Nothing else needs to exist."

live for *me*

"Call me when you get a divorce," I insisted.

"What do you want me to do? I can't make it go any faster. I don't have any feelings for her. Haven't I made it clear how much I love you?"

I wasn't looking for some sort of dramatic love vow from him. That wasn't the point. The point was when you blurred a line it ceased to exist in any way that mattered. So then the next go round you didn't even bother to draw it.

"You have. But you love me partially because I'm honest and that is what I'm doing here. I'm telling you the truth. Now is not the right time for us." I pulled open the door before I changed my mind.

I desperately wanted to say the hell with it and just turn and bury myself in his arms. But then who would I be? Devin Gold's girlfriend. Devin Gold's little girlfriend. Devin Gold's poor little girlfriend. I would be the person everyone looked at and felt sorry for, and eventually, some day, Devin would lose interest in me like I'd told Cat at Christmas. He could love me, but he could still lose interest in me if everything was always on his terms. I could only be with him if I were his partner, his equal, his wife.

So I ran. Because if I stopped to look at his face, to see the pain I was inflicting on him, feel the matching pain in my own heart, I would stay. And someday I would live to regret that choice.

He called after me. "Tiffany, wait! Be reasonable. Where the fuck are you even going?"

I had hit the elevator button and it dinged open immediately. I was on it, pushing L for lobby while he came down the hallway after me. As soon as he realized the elevator was already there he

224

swore and started running. The door was closing already and I was afraid he was going to stick his arm in it, but instead he just stood there, eyes locked on me, and let it close.

"Tiffany," he said. That's it. Just my name. Tears in his eyes.

And as the door closed entirely, blocking my view of him, I gave a choked sob.

Out on the sidewalk I asked the bellman for a cab and I got in, breathless, giving the driver the address on my phone. After a nauseating twenty minute ride we arrived in mid-town, at the office building of Randy Hart. My father. I didn't know what I thought I was going to do, but I gave the cab driver the majority of the cash I had in my purse. I hadn't been anticipating traveling. All I had was twenty dollars.

There was a seating area outside the building where employees smoked, and probably ate lunch in summer. But now it was briskly cold. Windy. I sat down on a bench next to a middle age woman shivering, cigarette up to her lips. I sat there for three hours, until my fingers went numb and my head spun. I hadn't eaten in twenty-four hours and I was still hurting from the wine. But I didn't have any money to buy lunch. Devin was blowing up my phone but I didn't answer his texts.

Finally around two, a man came out the front door. I knew instantly it was him. I'd seen his picture on social media. Had studied his features to see if I could see myself in him.

I stood up and approached him. He gave me a smile, but then said, "Look, I don't have any change for you."

He thought I was a panhandler. A homeless kid. He had a kind face, with warm brown eyes. He wasn't very old, and he was fit, handsome in his dress shirt and tie. "Are you Randy Hart?"

live for *me*

He frowned now. I rushed on before he went back into the building or called the cops on me. "Did you know a woman named Charlene Ennis? And have a daughter with her named Tiffany?" I reached out to steady myself on the concrete wall of the building. Everything was swaying now and I swallowed hard, the hot saliva in my mouth increasing.

"What the hell is this all about?" he asked cautiously.

"I'm Tiffany Ennis. I think I'm your daughter." I lost focus on him as everything in front of me went fuzzy, dark.

Then my knees buckled and I passed out cold.

chapter
fifteen

"THAT'S IT," MY FATHER SAID, taping a box shut. "Last box."

I smiled at him. "Thanks for helping me." There was very little I had wanted to keep in my grandmother's house, but I did decide to be practical and take dishes, glasses, towels with me back to Cat's. The rest had been donated to charity or thrown out, but it had been a big job dealing with it. My father had been there twice now helping me sort through stuff and I really appreciated it.

"It's the least I can do, hell." He gave me a rueful shrug.

The guilt he carried was substantial and I kept reassuring him none of it was his fault. To me all that mattered was knowing that if he had known about me, he would have taken me in. He still felt bad he hadn't verified my grandmother's story, but who the hell would think a grandmother would lie about her grandchild dying? Not anyone with a heart, that was for sure.

"It means a lot to me." I reached over and gave him a hug. The more time I'd spent with him, and his wife Tamara, the more of myself I'd seen in his features, his mannerisms. We had the same eyes, the same short build, the same laugh.

He held me tightly. He and Tamara had a four-year-old boy, my little half-brother, Tyrell, who was a bundle of energy and a sass master. He'd been just as accepting of me as his parents and when I looked at him, my heart melted. I had a family, though not in the traditional way. But it was good enough for me. It was more than I had ever expected.

Living with Cat and Heath was working out, short term, and I was starting college in the fall. I couldn't afford to live on my own, and while there was no market for rundown houses in Vinalhaven, I had managed to rent Gram's house to the new ferryboat operator, a single guy who didn't seem to care that it was a dump. He just liked the cheap rent. I liked the money in my pocket. Cat wasn't charging me rent but I knew someday I would pay her back. I'd have my LPN in less than two years and my father had offered to help me with tuition.

I felt more optimistic than I had since I'd first arrived at Richfield last fall.

It had been a hard winter. I had missed Devin every second of every day, but I had stood by my decision. I needed to establish my own life. I needed to step away from the drama of his life. I still had Google alerts on him and I saw what he was doing, what his friends were up to.

Cassandra had come out of rehab healthy and was back in the studio, according to the gossip sites. Sapphire had embarked on a summer tour. Lizzie and Alex had split up and she was dating a professional UFC fighter and planning a year-long stint in Vegas. Kadence was dating one of the owners of the Knicks and when she was frequently photographed courtside, she did not look pregnant.

Devin's divorce didn't seem to be final. I found no official filing of it in public court records.

There were a few pictures of him at music industry events and a mention of a beach vacation in February, with Jay and Sapphire. Nothing about him being involved with a woman.

He hadn't texted me. Not since the first week after I'd left him in the hallway outside the elevator.

And every day since I'd wondered if I'd done the right thing, while knowing that I had.

"Let's get these out to the car," Randy said.

I still couldn't quite bring myself to call him "dad." It felt forced. So for now I was calling him Randy. "Sounds good."

We stepped outside and I breathed in deeply. The June air was clean and warm. The old raspberry bush by the corner of the house had young fruit growing on it and I could practically taste the sweetness on my tongue. Funny how I had fantasized about fitting in in New York, but Maine was home. It just was. It was in me, and I wanted to stay there.

"What's that?" Randy asked, two boxes in his arms as we went down the steps to the gravel drive. "Looks like something is on fire over there."

I glanced in the direction he was pointing and my heart almost stopped. That was almost exactly where Richfield was. I knew because I had used the Internet to map out exactly where in relation to me Richfield was. The house wasn't visible from the island, but I had narrowed down the shoreline to the approximate location, and many a night had stood there, arms crossed, heart aching, staring across the ocean at it even though I'd known most likely Devin wasn't even there.

"That's a big fire," I commented. Smoke was billowing up rapidly, an angry black cloud. It had to be Richfield. That wasn't any other house in the area large enough to make a smoke cloud like that.

Pulling my phone out of my pocket, I called 911. I was sure someone else had reported it but I needed to know if I was right or wrong. I prayed I was wrong. "Yes, um, there's a fire on the mainland, halfway between town and the point. I just wanted to make sure someone has called it in already and trucks are on their way."

"Yes, we are aware of that fire, thank you."

"Where is it exactly? Are any roads closed?"

She rattled off the address. "Please stay out of the area so emergency vehicles can have access."

I murmured "thanks," then hung up. It was Richfield. On fire in a big, big way. I dropped the box I was holding on the ground and turned to Randy. "That's my old job, where I was housesitting. It's on fire."

I had told my father most of what had happened with Devin, other than that I had sex with him. I had been so upset and raw I hadn't been able to prevent myself from blurting it all out. Besides, Randy had wanted some kind of explanation for why I had fainted at his feet, nearly frozen solid.

"Seriously?" Randy popped the trunk of his car and put the

boxes in. "But Devin's not there, right? He's in the city most of the time."

"Yes. I mean, he wouldn't be there now. That's probably how the fire got so out of control. No one there to monitor it." But nonetheless I was still worried.

And the idea of the house I had fallen in love with being destroyed brought tears to my eyes. It was like none of it had ever happened then. Like I had never lived there. Like Devin and I hadn't had coffee and doughnuts in the kitchen. Like he hadn't taught me to drive there, like we hadn't cuddled on the couch with Amelia, or spent that one night together in my room off the kitchen.

I did what I hadn't done in six months. I texted Devin.

Where are you?

He didn't answer, even though I could see immediately he had read it. I realized it was coming out of nowhere so I typed a second text.

Richfield seems to be on fire. Are you safe?

Yes.

That was it. Just a yes.

Where are you?

Outside Richfield.

I had to go. There was no other option. "I have to go over there and make sure everything is okay. Devin says he's at the house." I felt sick to my stomach. If something had happened to him…

"Sure, okay. Let's catch the ferry. We can drop this stuff off at Caitlyn and Heath's first."

I glanced at the time. "Okay, great. Thank you."

live for *me*

"If he answered you, then clearly he's fine," Randy said, clearly wanting to reassure me.

"Yeah." I texted Devin again.

Please let me know what happens.

Sure.

That was it. Just a casual, cold response. Not that I could blame him. He hadn't heard from me at all.

As we waited for the ferry, took it across the water with a group of summer vacationers, and drove towards Devin's house, anxiety had my knee bouncing up and down. My palms were damp and I was biting my bottom lip. The smoke had decreased substantially which was either a good thing or a bad.

There were firetrucks everywhere. I expected someone to wave us away, but everyone was too busy. The fire was mostly out.

But the house was mostly gone. "Oh, my God," I breathed, tears in my eyes.

All that was still standing was the garage and half of the family room. The rest was nothing but a charred, smoldering heap. The garage door was open and sitting inside it was my jeep. The jeep I'd never driven. The blue paint was still visible below a layer of ash. He hadn't sold it back to the dealer or online. Scanning the yard, I looked for Devin.

He was sitting on a stretcher, waving off a paramedic and looking… defeated. It was an expression I'd only seen him wear once. On the other side of a closing elevator door. I ran. I just dropped my arms and ran. His hair was longer, but he looked gorgeous. My heart ached as I got closer and I slowed down, wanting to throw myself into his arms.

When he looked over and saw me, he froze. "What are you

doing here?" he asked tightly.

"I needed to make sure you were okay." I came to a stop in front of him. I was wearing flip flops that slid on the grass. "Are you okay?"

"I've been better." He gave a shrug. "But I'll live." When he lifted his hand off his stomach, I saw his shirt was open and he was bandaged. "I'm not sure why you care."

He sounded petulant and I couldn't blame him, but that wasn't my concern at the moment. I wanted to know how badly he was injured. "What happened? Did you get burned? How did the fire start?"

The paramedic was hovering and Devin turned to him. "Hey, can you give us a minute?"

"Sure. Don't go anywhere," he told Devin, clapping him on the leg.

"I promise not to run a marathon." When the man moved across the grass, Devin studied me. "You look beautiful, Tiffany." But then he shook his head, sighing in exasperation. "So is that what it takes to hear from you, my house burning to the ground?"

My bottom lip was trembling. "Why are you bandaged?"

"I may have gotten shot by Kadence."

"Oh, my God! *What?*" I couldn't stop myself. I reached out and pushed his hair back off his forehead. It was longer than it had been at Christmas. "She shot you? Why?"

He gave a shrug, moving his head away from my touch. "She was threatening to kill herself. I tried to stop her, she shot me. But it just grazed me. It hurts like a motherfucker but I'll be okay."

"I don't know what to say." But I did start crying. "If anything had happened to you…"

"You would be free to live your life without me," he said, gruffly. "Just like you have been."

"Don't say that. I don't want to be free of you. And if you suffer, I suffer."

"That's ironic, because I only suffer when you're not with me."

I touched him again, more confident now, both that he wasn't severely injured, and that while I was right to leave him the first time, it would be wrong to leave him again. "So let's not suffer anymore."

He didn't answer me though, just brooded. Happy to see him, happy to know that he had missed me, I kept talking. "So Kadence snowed me, didn't she?" The pictures, the doll, the pregnancy test, had all been a manipulation. I shivered when I thought about being alone with her. What she could have done to me. I wondered if she had been in Richfield without my knowing it. If she had watched me. It was disturbing and I felt like an idiot. It had taken her all of an hour to convince me she was sane, when she was clearly anything but.

"She's a sociopath, Tiff. She's good at lying. Pathologically good at it." He took my hand off his shoulder and kissed it, staring at me carefully. "We're officially divorced. Went to court yesterday and everything is filed."

That's what I had been waiting six months to hear. "Really? That's good news. I'm happy for you." I leaned closer to him. The air was acrid with smoke. "So where is she? Please tell me they arrested her."

"They did. Though they may conclude it was an accident. The arson, though? I don't think she can get out of that one. She threw gasoline all over everything. Funny thing is, she was trying to destroy your jeep. That TIFFANY license plate enraged her. But the jeep is still standing."

"Like you." Like me. Hopefully, even like us. I kissed his forehead, immensely relieved that he was okay. If she had shot him straight on and killed him, I didn't know what I would do.

"I don't know. I'm feeling kind of beat to shit. And I just lost about three million dollars between the house and everything in it. There wasn't any insurance on it. I let it lapse. Between that and the divorce settlement, I'm hard up for cash. I may need to sell the apartment in the village."

"I'm really sorry, Devin." I was. I knew he'd worked damn hard for everything he had. But I didn't doubt for a minute that he would recover. If he chose to.

"I'm a mess, Tiff. Broke. Busted." He briefly touched my waist. "You're wearing a dress," he said in a completely random comment.

"It's summer," I said, equally inane. "So where will you go if you sell the apartment in New York?"

"I think I'll rent for awhile. Maybe a small cottage on the coast here. Know a good housesitter?"

"Why do you need a housesitter if you'll be living there?" I asked, my voice low. I wanted to kiss him, desperately. I wanted to start over, on the same page. As partners. I couldn't walk away from him a second time. Not now that he was divorced. Not now that he had lost money, been injured. He needed me.

And I needed him.

"You tell me," he murmured. "Unless you have a boyfriend or something."

"No boyfriend. You?"

He shook his head. "No. No girlfriend either."

I laughed a little. "Well. I'd like to apply for the position of girlfriend since it's open. My qualifications are that I love you and I plan to never leave you."

"You're hired. Though I have to warn you I'm a hard employer. Demanding."

"I can handle it. I can handle you."

Devin started to move forward to kiss me but he winced in pain. So I met him halfway and pressed my lips to his. I was happy to meet him halfway. Happy to be his equal, his friend, his lover. God, I had missed him. His mouth felt perfect on mine, like we'd never been apart. When I moved back an inch, I breathed deeply, filling my nostrils with his scent.

"Can I start immediately?" I asked.

"I think you already have." Devin slipped his fingers into my hair and kissed me again, softly. "This doesn't seem like it's real. I didn't actually die, did I?"

The thought made me grip the sides of his shirt tightly. "No," I said tightly. "Of course not."

"I would die for you," he murmured to me. "Do you know that?"

"I don't want a man who will die for me, Devin." I rested my forehead on his. "I want a man who will live for me."

"I can do that, chipmunk." He smiled softly at me. "That's all I really want to do."

chapter
sixteen

S O WE RENTED THAT COTTAGE by the shore and I married him there. With my father and his family in attendance, Cat and Heath, and Devin's parents. We didn't want anyone else there, but it was perfect. We had lobster, blueberry salad, corn on the cob. There were fairy lights strung over the table on our back deck and lots of smiles and laughter. Tyrell ran around in circles, cramming blueberries into his mouth, and blowing bubbles with a bubble gun.

"So why did you get married?" he asked me in a tone like he thought I was crazy, climbing up on my lap.

"Because I love Devin," I told him, hugging his wiggling body against me.

"Duh." He rolled his eyes and moved his head back and forth.

I laughed. "Then why are you asking?"

"I don't know." He slid down off my lap again and blew

bubbles in Amelia's face, who bit them. Tyrell laughed as they popped over Amelia's snout.

Devin was sitting next to me and he reached over and gave me a kiss. He tasted like champagne. His amber eyes were full of mischief.

"What?" I asked him, suspicious, but smiling back. He looked very happy and that made me ecstatic.

"Look what just showed up." He pointed to the driveway of our cottage.

It was my jeep, fire ash cleaned off. It looked as perfect as it had in December. Only now I didn't feel strange about accepting it. Because I had a gift for him too.

"Thank you." I gave him a kiss. "You're very sweet."

"You'd better get your driver's license now or I'm selling it."

I stuck my tongue out at him. "I have a gift for you too." I jumped up out of my chair and went into the house to get it. I'd been hiding it in the cabinet above the fridge. Using a chair, I reached up there and retrieved the two boxes. My wedding dress brushed against my skin. It was just a simple off-the-rack strapless slip dress, but I felt beautiful and bridal in it.

"Don't fall," Cat said, coming into the kitchen.

"I'm fine."

"God, I can't believe you're married. You look beautiful, Tiffany."

I turned and gave her a wink. "Whatev."

She laughed. "Smartass. And to tell you the truth, I always knew you'd marry an older guy. You were way too worldly to settle for some twenty-year-old moron."

The thought made my skin crawl frankly. "Yeah, that was

never going to happen. I would have preferred to be single forever."

Cat smiled. "I'm just glad you're happy."

"Me, too. Look at us. Who would have thought?"

"Not me, that's for sure. We were dusty kids with hand-me-down clothes and scabs on our knees about a minute ago."

Cat's dark hair was pulled sleekly back in a high ponytail. It was a far cry from her teen years when it was always a snarled mess, half the time with twigs in it. "Ha. I was never dusty. That was you."

I hopped down on the chair, packages in hand. "It's your turn next."

"Tell Heath. He's the one who hasn't officially proposed to me. I'd say yes."

When we went outside, the men were gathered around the jeep in the driveway. Cat and I wandered over to join them.

"This is one awesome car," Randy said. "I think you should take your old man for a spin."

I laughed. "My temps are in my other dress." Actually, I wanted to drive Devin in it my first time on the road. I wanted to say thank you in a particularly private way. "But it's definitely awesome."

Devin stopped pointing out features to Heath and his own father long enough to hold his hand out for the present in my hand. "For me?"

"Yes." I gave him the small box.

He opened it and his eyes lit up. "A cupcake. Heck yeah."

"It's red velvet. Your favorite." And okay, so I had been cheesy enough to draw a heart on it by shaking sprinkles over a cookie cutter on top of the frosting. What could I say? I was in love.

"Thank you."

"The other one you can save for later." I held the bigger box up.

"Uh oh. Is that a dirty book? It's *Fifty Shades of Grey* and a pair of handcuffs, isn't it?" he teased.

"No!" Oh, my God, both our fathers were standing right there. "Don't be creepy at our wedding."

He laughed. "Sorry."

His mind was on sex, though. I knew it was. Just like mine. We hadn't been together since that one night in December and we were both really looking forward to our wedding night. His gunshot wound was healed now, and while that had been part of our reason for waiting, mostly it had been because we wanted to be husband and wife first. After everything, it just seemed more… special that way.

"I think I need a beer," Randy said.

"Me too," Mr. Gold agreed.

Devin laughed, but as soon as they walked back to the house with Heath, he took the box from me. "I'm dying of curiosity."

I suddenly felt nervous about it. "Maybe it's a dumb gift. I didn't really have any money, so…"

"Hey. I'm sure I'll love it." He opened the box and his nostrils flared. "It's your book. The one you were working on at Richfield."

"Yeah. I printed it out. I wanted you to be the first one to read it." I tried to express my feelings. "It wouldn't exist without you and your encouragement. So I thought you might like it."

"I'm sure I'll love it." He ran his fingers over the stack of paper. "This means a lot to me." His voice was tight.

"You mean a lot to me."

Devin was wearing a suit and he looked sexy as sin. He gave me a sly smile. "Show me later?"

"Deal."

S O AFTER EVERYONE LEFT, DEVIN and I decided to drive down to the beach. We could have walked, but I wanted to test out my jeep finally. He threw a blanket, the remains of the champagne, and some firewood into the back. "Should we change?" I asked.

"Nah. Let's make our wedding day last. I don't care if we get sandy."

The beach was private to only a half dozen houses and two of them weren't currently rented, so it was a safe bet we'd be alone down there.

When I hiked up my dress and jumped in my jeep I had to move the seat way up.

"Do you want a booster seat to sit on?" Devin asked.

"Be quiet." I turned the key and gave a little yell of triumph when it started. "OMG, this is so cool."

"Smile."

I turned and Devin had his camera up. He took a picture of me. "Let me see it. Do I look like butt?"

"No. You mostly definitely do not look like butt." He rolled his eyes. "Now show me your stuff, Mario Andretti."

I did officially have my temps but not my license, so it was legal for me to drive to the beach. Not that Devin would have cared, but I was something of a rule follower as I had discovered. I carefully drove us down the driveway, then down the road about a quarter of a mile to the small parking pad at the beach. The jeep bounced, but overall it was a smooth ride. I felt powerful driving it. Not the short girl any more but a woman with horsepower.

"I love this car."

"I love you."

Parking, I turned to him. "I love you, too."

"Let's walk on the beach, Tiffany Gold."

His words made me shiver. "Wow," I whispered. "That sounds amazing." I meant hearing my name. I knew that Cat intended to hyphenate her name some day, in honor of her father, but for me, Ennis was the name that belonged to two women who hadn't loved me well enough. So I didn't mind losing it. In fact, I loved having gained Devin's name. He was my family, what made me whole.

We held hands as we walked down to the water, Devin carrying the blanket. He spread it out. "Here, sit down, and I'll go back for the firewood."

I kicked off my sandals and sat down, staring out at the ocean, closing my eyes to breathe in the briny air and listen to the soft pounding of the waves on the beach. Devin came back and dug a hole and set up the wood. Within a few minutes we had a fire going. He sat down next to me and kicked off his shoes. He took a pull from the open champagne and handed it to me.

One sip was enough for me. I licked the bubbly sweetness off my lips. But Devin put his hand into my hair and drew me to him.

"Let me get that." He sucked my bottom lip. "Mmm. Tasty."

"That's what I was thinking. My husband is tasty," I murmured. I got a thrill from calling him that.

"My wife is tastier." He eased me back down onto the blanket.

The fire snapped next to us, light dancing over him as he stared down into my eyes. "What else should I taste?"

Desire made me languid, my breasts heavy, nipples hard. "I'm sure you can think of something."

His hand was on my waist, but it slipped lower, over my hip, my thigh. He tugged my dress up a little as he dropped his mouth onto my neck and kissed me. "Your skin is so smooth, so soft. I've dreamed about you, you know."

"What am I doing in your dreams?" I breathed, running my hands over his back, sneaking under his jacket to rake my nails across his dress shirt.

"Just what you are right now. You're looking up at me while I make love to you." His eyes were glassy and he sat back long enough to peel off his jacket and yank his shirt out of his pants.

"This is real." I wrapped my leg around the back of his calf and slipped my hand between us so I could stroke his erection through his pants.

"Right to business, huh? I'm not going to argue with that. It's been way too fucking long." Devin took his shirt off, tugged down his pants, and kicked them off into the sand. "Can I take your dress off?"

I glanced around. There was no one around near us. The lights from the nearest house seemed far enough away that they couldn't possibly see anything. And tonight, I wanted to be skin to skin with my husband. I nodded. "Yes." I sat up a little so he could unzip it and pull it over my head.

"Holy shit," he murmured, his hands running over my breasts, which were pushing out of the strapless bra.

live for *me*

It was the closet to cleavage I'd ever come. He sucked the swell of my flesh. "I approve this bra and these panties."

He caressed between my legs. The seamless panties were a low-cut thong. They outlined every inch of my body. But they were easy to slip to the side and when Devin's hand cupped me, I raised my hips and gave a moan of approval. I let him lead, kissing me everywhere, caressing every inch of me, mouth over my nipples first, then down to stroke across my moist heat.

When he slid into me, we both groaned. It was different than the first time. Still full, still invasive, but easy, instantly satisfying. There was no sting, just pure pleasure. He thrust while I gripped his tight ass and marveled at how good it felt.

"Hold onto me," he urged, and rolled us over, so that I wound up on top of him without him leaving my body.

For a second, I just lay there, swallowing hard, amazed at how wide open I was to him, how I could feel him pulsing deep inside me. "Oh, Devin," I breathed. "Oh, God."

"Move your hips, baby."

I wasn't lying flat on him but I wasn't sitting up either. I was halfway, my palms on the blanket on either side of his chest. I just looked down at him, not sure how to do that. Devin gripped my hips and started pumping up into me.

"Is this okay?" he asked.

It was basically the best thing that had ever happened to me. I was so shocked that I could only respond with a deep moan. The sensation built, spiraling out of my center, and I moved my hands onto his chest, digging my nails in, wanting to feel his muscles. Hold onto me.

When I came, it caught me by surprise. I arched my back as

shivers of pleasure rushed through me. Devin wasn't far behind. He thrust harder and then he was joining me. The shudders went on and on before I collapsed on his chest, arms shaky.

Devin kissed my temple. "I missed you so much. That felt amazing. You're amazing."

We lay there on the blanket, the fire beside us, the ocean waves in the background, both body and heart satisfied.

Home at last.

Thank you so much for reading *Live For Me*! Want to know when my next book is out? Sign up for my newsletter e-mail list at www.erinmccarthy.net/newsletter-2/

Want to know what happens next? Then turn the page for a special preview of *Let Me In (Blurred Lines #3)*

Hope you enjoy it!

let
me
in

(Blurred Lines #3)- Special Preview

W‍HAT'S WRONG?" CAT ASKED ME, turning towards me as I came into the living room.

"Nothing," I lied, putting my hand in my pocket so the stick wouldn't slide down out of my sleeve, where I had tucked it. "I'm going for a walk."

So I could cry and rage in private.

But she didn't believe me. She knew me too well.

"Aub, come on. You can tell me. Did you hear from Jared?"

I heard from Jared all the time. I had changed my number, but then he'd found me on social media. I'd blocked him, then he'd emailed me. No matter what I did, he found a way to track me down. A way to alternate between coaxing and cajoling me with pleas for me to come home, vows of love, and scathing condemnations on my character. How a man could claim he loved me and turn around and call me a dick-sucking whore was something I would never understand. Then again, how could a man who loved me knock out my teeth and leave me bleeding on the floor?

But this anxiety wasn't about a communication from Jared.

It was about what I'd been suspecting but was determined to ignore.

"I haven't heard from Jared today. I just want to take a walk. Am I allowed to do that?" I sounded bitchy and I knew it, but I needed to get away, to escape.

Living with Cat and her boyfriend, Heath, for the last month had allowed me time to think, feel, heal. I was grateful to both of them for taking me in when I hadn't been able to face my family with the shame of what had been done to me, what I had become. I owed Cat everything for hiding me, helping me to feel safe, not pressuring me to make decisions, and listening to me when I needed to talk.

I wasn't ready to share this yet though. I wasn't even ready to admit it.

Her look was one of sympathy, which made me feel worse. I was the girl everyone felt sorry for. That was the identity Jared had created for me.

"Of course you can do that. I just don't want you to keep everything bottled up. You can tell me anything."

"You just don't want me to throw myself off a cliff," I said dryly, leaning over the back of the couch and giving her a hug from behind. "For which I thank you. No worries. I'm not suicidal."

I wasn't. The opposite in fact. Staring into Jared's eyes, seeing his rage, had made me realize just exactly how much I wanted to live.

Even now, even with this, I wanted to survive more than

anything. I wanted to reclaim my life, find me again. Or at least a new version of me.

She leaned forward and glanced up at me over her shoulder. "I still can't get over your hair." She touched the ends of loose, auburn strands. "It's so different now that you dyed it."

I was a natural blonde, but that didn't feel right anymore. There was nothing carefree and beachy about the way I moved, always glancing over my shoulder, keeping my mouth closed as much as possible, self-conscious of the two missing teeth on the back right side. Dark auburn suited me better. It was moody, mysterious. It made my skin seem pale, and that was how I felt. Pale. Fragile.

"Redheads are feisty," I said. "I'm trying to find my inner feisty."

"You've always been feisty. And the master of sarcasm."

Not anymore. Cat had been living on an island off the coast of Maine for the last eighteen months. She'd never seen me with Jared. I was glad. The less witnesses to my humiliation the better, and maybe with her seeing me as I had been, I would become me again.

"I think the feisty got knocked out of me. Literally."

"Don't joke about it." Her dark eyes searched mine. "I don't think that's healthy."

Nothing about it was healthy. But I was trying my best to cope. And when she looked at me like that…that's when I needed to escape.

"I'll be back in an hour tops. Don't send Heath out looking for me again. I promise I'll be fine."

That was why I'd come to Cat in Vinalhaven—it was remote,

isolated. Everyone knew everyone, and the only way on the island was by ferry. If, for some insane reason, Jared tried to track me down, I would know immediately that he was there. It made me feel safe, protected. Walking helped clear my head.

The porch door slammed behind me, and I put the hood of my sweatshirt up. It was only September, but I was always cold. I used to think I would go to grad school down South. Now, the future was a great gaping hole filled with fear.

And a baby.

I fingered the stick stuck up my sleeve and tried to process the truth. I was pregnant. With Jared's baby. Tears filled my eyes as I walked down the gravel drive towards the shoreline, my feet moving faster, my head hunched down. Heading in the direction of the least possibility of seeing any other humans, I cursed when I realized almost immediately that the guy who lived in a crumbling farmhouse was out in his yard. Chopping wood with his shirt off. He was in his mid-twenties and I'd seen him twice before. He never smiled, he never waved, he never spoke to me, and he was muscular, ominous. There was no joy on his face, only a kind of silent disdain as he watched me walk by. He was the kind of man who could corner me, beat me, rape me, kill me.

Five years ago, I would have seen his sweaty shoulders, watched the ripple of muscles in his back, and I would have flirted with him, smiled, flipped my hair. He might have flirted back and we might have gone into his farmhouse and fucked just because it felt good. Now, the thought of him touching me made me flinch in fear, and I rushed past him, glancing up only to track his movements, make sure he wasn't following me.

Cat had said that his name was Riker and he was harmless.

That he'd come back from being in the military and he had PTSD, so he kept to himself. Riker was sweet, she'd insisted. He had always been a good guy.

Whatever. What he was then didn't make him that now, and I was afraid of the intensity of his stare.

He was doing it now. His ax paused as he eyed me. Then his gaze shifted back to the log and the sun hit the blade as it came down with a violent whack. I winced. The wood split in two directions and tumbled to the ground.

Suddenly, it was too much—the realization that a guy forty feet away could frighten me, that I was pregnant, that I had let myself get in this situation by wanting so desperately to be important to Jared in the beginning that I had ignored all the warning signs. I started to run, wondering how I was going to support myself and a child, afraid that if Jared ever found out, he would take my baby away from me. Knowing that, at some point, I had to face my family.

I ran, pumping my arms hard, the hood falling back off my head, my lungs straining. When I reached the edge of the island by the rocks, I came to a crashing halt, sobbing in frustration. Yanking the pregnancy test out of my sleeve, I stared at the pink line showing my new reality.

"It's not fair," I whispered.

I'd always wanted to be a mom. But not like this. Not with *that* man.

"No," I said, louder this time. "No. This isn't fair!" Then I pulled my arm back and hurled the test stick as hard as I possibly could.

I was panting, my vision blurry from tears as I watched it sail through the air and drop down onto the rocks. Leaning forward to see where it landed, I slipped on the wet turf.

Suddenly, I was falling and screaming and trying to grab on to anything. Pain shot through my hip, but clipping the rock helped slow my fall and I landed on my chest, my legs dangling, my grip tenuous, but no longer free falling. The air whooshed out of my lungs and I clawed at the slippery rock with my feet, trying to find a ledge to haul myself up. But my shoes slid around uselessly and I paused, panting, arms straining. I was wasting too much energy and I needed to think.

Looking up, I opened my mouth to scream for help.

What I saw almost made me lose my hold entirely.

A man's face stared down at me with dark, intense eyes.

Riker.

about the author

USA Today and New York Times Bestselling author Erin McCarthy sold her first book in 2002 and has since written almost sixty novels and novellas in teen fiction, new adult, and adult romance. Erin has a special weakness for New Orleans, tattoos, high-heeled boots, beaches and martinis. She lives in Florida with her husband, a grumpy cat and a socially awkward dog.

You can find Erin on Facebook, Twitter, or on Goodreads. Also don't forget to visit her website at www.erinmccarthy.net.

Made in United States
North Haven, CT
15 February 2022

16153115R00157